DOCTOR WHO AND THE FACE OF EVIL

DOCTOR WHO
AND THE
FACE OF EVIL

Based on the BBC television serial *The Face of Evil* by
Chris Boucher by arrangement with the British
Broadcasting Corporation

TERRANCE DICKS

Number 25 in the Doctor Who Library

published by
the paperback division of
W. H. Allen & Co. Ltd

A Target Book
Published in 1978
by the Paperback Division of W. H. Allen & Co. Ltd
A Howard & Wyndham Company
44 Hill Street, London W1X 8LB

Reprinted 1979
Reprinted 1980
Reprinted 1982
Reprinted 1983

Printed and bound in Great Britain by
Cox & Wyman Ltd, Reading

ISBN 0 426 20006 3

Contents

1

The Outcast

The Sevateem were holding a trial.

The big Council hut was packed with elders and warriors. Andor, Chief of the Tribe, sat on his throne of shining metal. Around him stood his Councillors, Tomas, Calib and Sole. In the shadows behind the throne waited Neeva, Shaman, Witch Doctor, Speaker of the Law.

It was a colourful, barbaric scene. Light from a ring of smoking torches made the great Council hut bright as day. It glinted from the weapons of the savage skin-clad warriors and the strange regalia of the elders. It blazed fiercely on the prisoner who stood before the throne, flanked by crossbow-carrying guards.

The prisoner was a girl called Leela. She was tall, with brown hair and dark eyes, a broad clear forehead and a firm chin. Her arms and legs, exposed by her brief skin costume, were brown and smoothly muscular. She stood before her accusers wary but unafraid, like a captured wild animal.

Calib had taken on the role of prosecutor. He was a wiry, thin-faced man, his handsome features marred by an air of cunning. He turned dramatically towards the Chief, as he concluded his speech of accusation. 'You are our leader, Andor, and you know the Law.

There can be but one punishment for such an offence as this. She must be banished.'

There was a growl of agreement from the crowd. Yet some were silent, out of sympathy for the prisoner. The sentence of banishment was a sentence of death. The offender would be cast out, into the Beyond. Who could hope to survive without the protection of the Tribe?

Andor tugged thoughtfully at his grizzled beard. He was a stocky man in his fifties, a grim experienced warrior. He had fought his way to the throne by strength and ruthless cunning. There was no succession by right in the Tribe of Sevateem. The shining throne, handed down from the Old Time, belonged to the man who could take it—and keep it. He turned to Sole, his Chief Councillor, and said, 'What say you, Sole?'

Sole, a man much like Andor himself, stared grimly ahead. 'You should not ask, Andor. The Law is the Law.' Andor had expected such an answer from his old friend—even though Leela was Sole's daughter.

Andor looked at the prisoner, who returned his gaze proudly. Such a pity, he thought. She was a fine strong girl, one of the bravest and fiercest of his warriors. Soon she would have married and had fine sons and daughters to serve the Tribe. Andor had noticed that Tomas, youngest of his Council, spent much time with Leela. Now the girl had condemned herself, by her own rashness. 'The Council is agreed,' said Andor gruffly. 'Leela must be sent Beyond.'

Impulsively Tomas stepped forward. 'No, Andor, pardon her. She is young.'

'Do not beg, Tomas,' said Leela fiercely. 'What I said was truth.'

Neeva stepped out from behind the throne, into the torch-light. He was a small man, with a smooth, ageless face. His head was shaved to denote his priestly rank. His ceremonial robe hung from his shoulders. It was a strange, silvery garment, all in one piece, with arms and legs and a round helmet at the neck. It was a sacred relic of the Old Time, and Neeva wore it draped over his shoulders like a cloak.

Neeva was a figure of great authority in the Tribe, second only to Andor himself. There was a respectful hush as he spoke. 'The girl is a blasphemer. She has profaned the holy purpose of the Tribe of Sevateem.'

Leela seemed determined to condemn herself. 'Holy purpose? To die for nothing in another useless attack?'

'The god Xoanon demands she be cast out,' said Neeva angrily. 'He told me this!'

'Liar!' snapped Leela. 'There *is* no Xoanon!'

There was a shocked murmuring from the Tribe. Neeva spread out his hands. 'Blasphemy,' he said triumphantly.

Andor looked at Leela's proud face, and at the impassive features of her father. There was nothing he could do for her now. She had condemned herself before all the Tribe. Yet there was one faint hope of life he could offer her—life or a quicker death. 'Leela! Will you take the Test of the Horda?'

Silently Leela shook her head. Better the unknown terrors of the Beyond than death in the Pit of the Horda.

Andor looked round the crowded hut. 'Will any take it for her?'

No one moved or spoke. Many warriors had looked with favour on Leela. But life was precious, and after all, there were other women. Andor looked at Tomas, who dropped his eyes in shame. Even his love was not strong enough to face almost-certain death.

'*I* will take the Test.' Sole left his place and came to stand before the throne.

'No,' shouted Leela. 'You'll be killed——'

'Be silent, daughter,' commanded Sole. 'You have said enough.'

Andor raised a commanding hand. 'Test him!' Two guards led Sole away.

Leela could face the prospect of her own death unafraid, but the thought that her rashness would destroy her father was more than she could bear. She fell to her knees before the throne. 'Andor, please. Don't let him ... Call them back!' She looked up at Neeva. 'Great Shaman, Speaker of the Law, I was wrong to speak as I did. Forgive me, please, *please* ...'

Andor leaned forward on his throne. 'Be silent, girl. Your father is a warrior. Do not shame him.'

There was a long, long silence. Leela got slowly to her feet, brushing tears from her eyes as if ashamed of her outburst.

The silence was broken at last by a brief scream of agony from the outskirts of the village. Leela bowed her head, touching throat, left shoulder and left hip in a ritual gesture. Many others in the Council hut did the same.

Andor rose and pronounced sentence. 'Outcast of

the Tribe of Sevateem be gone from us.'

Neeva's voice rose in a kind of chant. 'Spawn of the Evil One, return to your Master!'

'You have until sunrise,' said Andor sternly. 'If, by then, you are still within the Boundary, you will be thrown to the Horda.'

Leela turned and walked away. The crowd drew apart to let her pass. She was unclean now, accursed, an outcast from the tribe.

Tomas stood silent, head bowed in shame. He should have taken the Test of the Horda. Yet what would have been the use? Not one in a hundred survived the Test. Besides, Leela *was* guilty, she had blasphemed the Law of the Tribe. Tomas looked up and saw Neeva deep in conversation with two of his acolytes—young warrior priests who had been chosen to serve him. The warriors hurried out of the hut clearly following Leela. Tomas watched them leave, and then set off after them. Perhaps he could still do something for Leela after all.

In a forest clearing, not very far away, a strange, wheezing groaning sound broke the silence and a square blue shape materialised beneath the mighty trees. A door opened and a tall curly-haired man stepped out. He wore loose, comfortable clothes with a vaguely Bohemian air. A broad-brimmed soft hat was jammed on the back of a tangle of curly hair, and an incredibly long scarf dangled round his neck.

The Doctor stood staring rather bemusedly about him, as if not sure where he was, or what he was doing

11

there. The most recent events seemed vague and remote in his mind. He'd defeated the Master's diabolical scheme to destroy the Time Lord planet of Gallifrey. Then he'd set course for Earth. Or had he? Had his fingers sent the TARDIS to some other destination, guided by some impulse deep in his unconscious mind.

The Doctor looked around. He was in a small clearing in a huge primeval forest. Giant trees towered around him in all directions, cutting off most of the light from the sky. The trees were festooned with dangling vines, dense shrubs and bushes filled the space between tree trunks and there was a deep, soft carpet of leaves beneath his feet. 'Not Hyde Park, I think,' muttered the Doctor. 'Could be a nexial discontinuity, I suppose. I really must remember to overhaul that Tracer. I'll put a knot in my hanky ...' He groped in his pockets and produced a red-spotted handkerchief—with a knot in one corner. 'I wonder what that was for?' The Doctor scratched his head, feeling that things were getting away from him. It was as if some long-buried memory was trying to push its way to the surface. Somehow this place was familiar ...

The Doctor shrugged. If he had brought himself back here for some purpose there was only one way to find out. 'Little look round, Doctor?' he murmured. 'Why not?'

He set off into the forest then stopped with an obscure feeling of something missing. Of course! Sarah Jane Smith. She should have been beside him as usual, grumbling about their unexpected arrival in a strange destination, and the dangers they were sure to meet. The Doctor gave a rueful smile. Sarah was back on Earth now, like Harry Sullivan and the Brigadier. It had been the Doctor's own decision to take her back. Time Lord law had prevented him from taking her to Gallifrey. Besides, it was more than time that she took up her own ordinary human life again. Yes, the Doctor decided, he'd acted for the best. But as he walked through the forest, he couldn't help feeling a little lonely ...

Leela moved cautiously ahead, crossbow at the ready. She was still inside the Boundary, but despite this all her hunter's instincts were on the alert. There were noises not far behind her. Disturbed shrubbery whispering back into place, the crackle of dry leaves underfoot. Tiny, almost inaudible sounds, but to Leela they told a clear story. Something was tracking her.

She came to a kind of natural road through the forest. It stretched at right angles in front of her, barring her way. Leela hesitated. She had to cross it—but the moment she stepped into the open she would be exposed to her pursuer. Since there was no alternative, Leela took a cautious step into the open. Higher up the glade to her right, someone else did exactly the same thing. It was one of Neeva's temple guards, crossbow in hand.

For a fraction of a second they confronted each other in mutual astonishment. The guard whipped up his crossbow. Leela's bow was aimed and ready, and she fired first. The guard reeled back and fell, a crossbow bolt through his heart.

With the instinct of long training Leela instantly reloaded her crossbow, slotting in a new bolt and forcing back the heavy metal spring that powered it. Just as the spring clicked into place she heard a rustling to her left. A second guard had stepped from cover. Now positions were reversed. His weapon was aimed and ready, hers still pointing downwards. Even as she raised her bow to fire Leela knew she was doomed. There was the twang of a crossbow spring— and the guard fell face down, a bolt between his shoulder-blades.

Tomas stepped forward, bow in hand.

Leela stared at him. 'Tomas! What are you doing here?'

He stepped over the body of the guard and came towards her. 'I've come to take you back.'

'You know I can't do that.'

'Don't you see?' interrupted Tomas. 'I saw Neeva send those guards. He doesn't trust his own prophecies. We can tell the Council, discredit him.'

'It wouldn't make any difference ... not now.'

'Leela, you can't cross the Boundary.'

'They haven't left me much choice.'

'But you'll be killed. There are phantoms in the Beyond.'

'Feast-fire stories,' said Leela scornfully.

'There's something there,' insisted Tomas. 'No one who crosses the Boundary ever comes back.'

Leela was silent for a moment. For all her bravado she knew Tomas was right. Then she said resolutely,

'Well, whatever's there I'll face it. I can take care of myself.'

'Then I'll go with you.'

Leela looked affectionately at him. She was fond of Tomas and didn't blame him for refusing to take the Test for her. By speaking out against Xoanon she had outraged his deepest beliefs, and she was touched by his offer to join her in exile. But it was too late to turn back now—for either of them. 'No,' she said fiercely. 'Go back to the Tribe. I'm going now. Goodbye.'

She moved away, and Tomas stood staring disconsolately after her. Leela crossed the ride, then turned back for a final word of warning. 'Beware of the devious Calib. One day he'll get so cunning even he won't know what he's planning!' She disappeared into the trees on the other side.

Tomas gazed after her a moment longer, then turned and began his journey back to the village.

Somehow Leela knew when she came to the Boundary. It was nothing you could see or touch. Rather it was something you felt, a kind of tingling in the air. It didn't prevent you from going on, but it made every instinct scream to turn and go back. It took all her courage to press on, but she persisted, and a moment later the feeling faded. She had crossed the Boundary. She was in the Beyond.

Leela looked round, half-expecting monsters to spring out of nowhere—but nothing happened. The forest on one side of the invisible barrier looked exactly like that on the other. But somehow it felt different, she decided. It was silent, menacing. It seemed to be waiting. Uneasily she moved on.

Leela had no plan in mind. Since no one had ever returned from the Beyond she had no idea what to expect. Presumably there was game in this part of the forest too, so she would be able to survive. Perhaps there was some other tribe that would take her in. If she tried to return to the Sevateem they would kill her. Neeva would see to that. By attacking the god Xoanon she was attacking him, and Neeva had acted with typical ruthlessness to dispose of the threat. His attempt had failed, thanks to Tomas. But Leela knew she would not live long if she ever returned within Neeva's reach.

Then she heard the noise of pursuit. Not furtive rustling sounds this time but the arrogant crashing of some great beast too powerful to need to conceal its presence. She started to run, and the sounds came after her. She broke into a panic-stricken flight, and the trampling sound followed her through the forest.

She came to another glade and ran across it. On the other side, she paused and turned round. She had to know what was hunting her. Judging by the volume of the noise it was making the creature must be enormous, towering above the trees. Leela turned and saw —nothing. But the sound was still there, and coming closer. She saw branches thrust aside, undergrowth trampled flat by the passage of some enormous bulk. Then a line of colossal footprints appeared, moving across the clearing towards her. She was being hunted through the forest by an invisible monster ...

2

The Invisible Terror

The trouble with forests, decided the Doctor, is that they are undoubtedly rather monotonous. The vine-festooned trees stretched away in every direction, their spreading leaves combining to make a dense green roof. A kind of straggling trail led through the low-lying bushes. The only sound was the crackle of dry leaves underfoot. Occasionally a clearing gave a brief glimpse of the sky, and beyond the clearings were yet more trees.

The Doctor considered returning to the TARDIS and trying some other planet. But he couldn't rid himself of the feeling that there was some purpose in his coming to this place. He strode on through the silent forest, hoping that this purpose, if there was one, would soon be revealed.

He heard someone moving towards him. The Doctor stood still, and waited. A tall brown-haired girl in a brief costume made of animal skins came haring through the trees. She tripped over a projecting tree-root and tumbled at his feet. Instinctively the Doctor moved forward to help her up. When she saw him looming over her she gave a gasp or horror.

He took her hand and helped her to her feet. 'Hello, did I startle you?'

The girl shrank back. Strange, thought the Doctor, she didn't look the nervous type. Why was she so frightened of him? He smiled reassuringly and said, 'Don't worry, I won't hurt you.'

'The Evil One,' breathed the girl fearfully.

The Doctor was used to unfriendly receptions, but this kind of terror was going too far.

'Well, nobody's perfect, but that's overstating it a bit. I'm the Doctor. What's your name?'

'Leela.' Still the same hesitant whisper.

The Doctor tried to think of some way to reassure her. 'Leela,' he said soothingly. 'That's a nice name. I've never met anybody called Leela.' He fished a crumpled paper bag from his pocket. 'Would you like a jelly baby, Leela?'

The girl gave a gasp of horror. 'It's true then! They used to tell us the Evil One eats babies.' She made a curious ritual gesture touching throat, left shoulder and left hip.

'You mustn't believe all they tell you. Actually these are sweets ... Have one, they're rather good.'

The girl shook her head, staring at the bag as if it contained unimaginable horrors. All at once the forest around them seemed to come alive. Trees began shaking, the ground quivered, and from every direction there came a massive trampling sound, and a noise of deep hoarse breathing.

The Doctor looked enquiringly at Leela. 'Either you have some very large friends with very bad colds, or we're in trouble,' he said conversationally. 'Now, which is it?'

'They are the Monsters of the Beyond. They are your creatures.'

'They are? I wonder if they know that. What do they look like?'

'They cannot be seen. They are phantoms.'

'Invisible? Then we've got a chance.' Putting his jelly babies away the Doctor dug deeper into his pockets and produced a rather ancient-looking mechanical device.

'A magic talisman?' asked Leela reverently.

'No, a clockwork egg-timer.' The Doctor began winding up the device, chatting quietly as he did so, apparently quite unworried by the thunderous approach of the monsters. 'The visible spectrum will be largely irrelevant to our invisible friends. They're virtually blind.'

'Then how do they find us?'

'Roughly speaking, they home in on our vibrations.' The Doctor carried the egg-timer over to the rocks and jammed it in a crevice. 'Now, Leela, I want you to do exactly what I say. We're going to move away, very slowly and very quietly. No matter what happens, you mustn't cry out or make any sudden move. And don't run till I tell you. Is that clear?'

Leela looked at him in puzzlement. If this really was the Evil One, why was he going to such trouble to save her from his own creatures? She decided it was safer not to argue—she could always escape later.

She nodded and the Doctor said, 'Good. Come on!' He took Leela's hand and they began creeping away. The crashing, trampling sounds were very close now, as if one of the monsters had moved ahead of the rest.

Suddenly the Doctor said, 'Freeze!' and stood quite still looking behind him.

'What's the matter?'

'Sssh! We must tread very carefully!' Still looking over his shoulder the Doctor took a step forward, tripped over a trailing vine and fell flat on his face.

Immediately there was a tremendous commotion as the invisible monster came pounding even closer. Leela saw a line of enormous footprints appearing on the forest floor—footprints heading straight towards them. Terror-struck she turned to run, but a discordant jangling rang out. It was the bell on the egg-timer. Immediately the footprints veered, making their way towards this sound.

The Doctor scrambled to his feet. 'Saved by the bell! Come on!' There came a crash from behind them, and the ringing of the bell was cut off. Leela turned and looked. Some invisible force had shattered the egg-timer into tiny fragments. Now great fountains of earth were being thrown up and even the rocks themselves hurled through the air in fragments, smashed to pieces by the invisible monster's fury. Leela shuddered, and hurried off after the Doctor.

In the Council hut, Tomas was pleading Leela's cause to Calib. 'I tell you Neeva sent two guards in secret to kill her.'

Calib stood silent, considering the information. Already his cunning mind was seeking ways to turn this incident to his advantage.

'Well, if you're not interested,' said Tomas angrily.

'But I *am* interested. What happened?'

'They failed. Leela killed one, I killed the other.'

20

Calib nodded thoughtfully. 'Neeva is beginning to make mistakes.'

'We must call a meeting of the Council, and tell them.'

'Tell them what?'

'Leela was delivered to the judgement of Xoanon. Her sentence was banishment, not execution. Neeva has broken his own Law.'

'Don't be naïve, Tomas.' Calib was an experienced politician. 'Even if the Council believed you, don't you think Neeva would have an answer? He's the Speaker of the Law. He'd say Xoanon *told* him to send the guards.'

Tomas said despairingly, 'There must be something we can do.'

'There is. Neeva has *promised* us victory in the next raid across the Barrier. He says Xoanon has told him that this time we will win. You see what that means?'

'If we don't win . . .' said Tomas slowly.

'Exactly. Neeva's going to look like the charlatan he is. Then we can move against him—and that old fool Andor.' There was no doubt in Calib's mind as to who was going to be the new Chief.

Tomas wasn't interested in Calib's intrigues. 'By then a lot of good men will have died, Calib. We should stop the raid.'

'Like Leela?'

Tomas sighed. 'Yes, she tried, didn't she? And by now she's probably dead.'

Leela felt the strange tingling in the air, forced her

way through it, and came to a halt. 'We can rest now. We're safe.'

The Doctor came to join her. 'How can you be so sure?'

'We're back inside the Boundary. Didn't you feel it?'

'I certainly felt something,' said the Doctor. 'You're sure those creatures won't follow?'

'They never cross the Boundary. *You* should know that.'

'I keep telling you, Leela, I'm *not* the Evil One. Who saved your life, eh?'

'You did,' agreed Leela meekly. She still wasn't sure what to make of her strange companion. He *looked* like the Evil One. But why didn't he *act* like him? And it was certainly true that he'd saved her life. Without him she'd have been crushed by the invisible monsters. Perhaps the Evil One was toying with her, saving her for some even more horrible fate ... Yet somehow Leela doubted it. She had an instinct for danger, and sensed that the Doctor didn't mean her any harm.

The Doctor was looking back the way they'd come. 'Never cross the Boundary, eh? I'm sure those things don't stay over there out of a sense of fair play. This must be a fence of some kind.'

'A fence?'

'That's right. An invisible fence—for invisible monsters!' The Doctor started poking around in the bushes.

In the Inner Sanctum, Neeva knelt before the altar of Xoanon. The Sanctum formed a walled-off corner of the Council hut. It was filled with holy relics including a selection of strange and mysterious objects arranged upon the wooden altar. A technologically-minded person would have recognised, among other things, a disruptor gun, a space ship's medikit, a portable communicator, and an ultra-beam accelerator. But to Neeva, and indeed to all the Tribe of Sevateem, these were the holy relics of Xoanon, their purpose, if they had one, shrouded in sacred mystery.

Neeva knelt before the altar, head bowed, waiting for his god to speak.

Xoanon's voice, as always, seemed to come out of the air. 'Neeva,' it whispered eerily. 'Neeva, are you listening?'

'Speak, Lord, your servant hears.'

'The girl Leela has returned across the Boundary, with a companion. You have failed me.'

'Oh great god, Xoanon, I have faithfully done all that you have commanded.'

'You crawling thing, do you presume to argue?'

Neeva abased himself. 'No, Lord. Forgive me.'

'Hear this, Neeva. The girl Leela, and the one who is with her must be destroyed. *See that it is done.*'

3

Captured

It took the Doctor quite a long time to discover what he was looking for, but he found it at last, hidden beneath the roots of a dense clump of bushes. It was a plain black box with a rhythmically-flashing light set into the top. 'Just as I thought, a low-intensity sonic disruptor, set for a hundred and eighty-degree spread.'

Leela looked at the box in awe. 'That keeps away the phantoms?'

'Gives them a nasty headache if they get too close.' Replacing the box, the Doctor straightened up. 'There must be others set at intervals all along the Boundary.' He looked thoughtfully at Leela. 'The technology's very advanced. So your people didn't put them there——'

Leela made the ritual gesture of protection. 'Xoanon,' she said reverently.

'Xoanon? Who are they?'

'Xoanon is Xoanon. He is worshipped by the Tribe of Sevateem. They cast me out for speaking against him. It is said that he is held captive ...'

'Really? By the Evil One, I presume?'

Leela nodded. 'And by his followers, the Tesh.' Leela's head was whirling with speculations. 'Maybe Neeva is right. Perhaps there is a holy purpose. I just don't know what to believe any more.'

'That's a healthy sign. Never be too certain of any-thing, Leela, it's a sign of limited intelligence. And just where is Xoanon supposed to be held captive?'

Leela's reply came in a kind of ritualised chant. 'Within the Black Wall, wherein lies Paradise.'

'Is that just religious gobbledygook? Or is there an actual place?'

'There is the Wall.'

'Is there? Splendid. Show me.'

Leela stared at him. Surely the stranger couldn't be the Evil One, or he wouldn't need to be shown the Wall he himself had made. Or was it all a trick? Still very much on her guard, Leela led the way through the forest.

'Why?' demanded Andor angrily. 'Why has the game disappeared from the forest? Where is the love of Xoanon for his people? Where is your magic, Neeva?'

Neeva looked up at the angry figure on the throne. 'Xoanon knows that there are those amongst the Tribe who do not wish to fight.'

'And so he starves us?'

'How can he bless those who do not love him? There will be food for those who brave the Wall in his name.'

'Men do not fight well on empty stomachs,' growled Andor.

Neeva's voice was calm, persuasive, totally assured. 'Soon the gap in the Wall will appear. Then you will summon the warriors and I will speak the Litany before the attack. I will tell you when it is time.'

Andor waved dismissively. 'Go! And do not delay too long.'

Neeva inclined his head—not the bow of a servant to his king but a nod between equals—and returned to his Sanctum. Andor watched him go, his face heavy with rage. Always the same smooth answers, the well-rehearsed reciting of the Law. Meanwhile the Tribe went hungry, and there were those who plotted against him. Andor knew that unless Neeva's promises were fulfilled, unless there was food and victory soon, the Sevateem would demand a new chief.

His gloomy reflections were interrupted by Tomas who strode abruptly into the Council hut and bowed before the throne. 'Well, Tomas?' growled Andor.

'There is something I must say.'

'Then say it, boy.'

'I agree with Leela—about the attack. It's madness. It will be just like all the other times. Many of us will die, and we shall achieve nothing.'

'Nevertheless, we shall attack. It is the will of Xoanon.'

'We have only Neeva's word for that.'

(Alerted by the mention of his name Neeva moved closer to the door of the Sanctum.)

Andor climbed stiffly from his throne and put a massive hand on Tomas's shoulders. 'You must have faith, my son.'

'In the word of a murderer? Neeva sent men in secret to kill Leela. Or did you already know that?'

'Watch your tongue, boy,' said Andor roughly. 'Don't let me hear you speak against the attack again. We

26

shall strive to free Xoanon from the Tesh. And we shall do it together, as one people.'

Tomas bowed his head in resignation. 'Yes, Andor,' he said, and allowed Andor to lead him from the hut.

Neeva watched them from the Sanctum. Something would have to be done about Tomas, he decided.

The Doctor strode abstractedly through the forest, his mind still worrying at long-buried memories. Xoanon! Why was that name so familiar to him? He'd never been to this planet before. Or had he?

All at once he realised Leela had disappeared. One minute she was beside him, the next she was gone. He looked round. 'Leela, where are you?' He heard her voice from somewhere about knee level.

'Doctor, get under cover. Quickly, I thought I heard something.' Leela had hidden inside a clump of bushes at the base of a giant tree. She crouched perfectly still, merging with her surroundings like a wild animal.

'Leela, we don't have time to play games.'

'You don't understand ...'

'No, no, *you* don't understand,' said the Doctor tolerantly. 'Look, if they're all busy preparing for this attack on the Wall, they're scarcely likely to send patrols out just on the off-chance that you might come back.'

The Doctor beamed, pleased with his own impeccable logic, and two crossbow bolts thudded into the tree beside him. 'Of course,' he continued thoughtfully, 'I could be wrong about that!'

27

From somewhere in the trees a voice shouted, 'You, stand still.'

'Oh absolutely,' called the Doctor. Without looking round he hissed, 'Leela, I don't think they've spotted you. Stay out of sight—and get moving.'

'I can't leave you. They'll kill you.'

'*Go away,*' whispered the Doctor urgently. He heard the rustle of movement behind him, and a harsh voice said, 'You! Who are you?'

'I'm the Doctor. Who are *you*—and why are you shooting at me?'

'Where's Leela?'

'Who?' asked the Doctor innocently.

'Spread out and search,' ordered the voice. 'She must be round here somewhere.'

Before the warriors could obey, the Doctor said quickly, 'Would you mind terribly if I turned round? I feel a bit silly talking to this tree.' Without waiting for a reply, the Doctor turned. Four crossbow-carrying warriors were grouped round him in a semicircle. As they saw his face they instinctively fell back, each one making the ritual sign of protection. 'The Evil One,' whispered their leader.

The Doctor started walking towards them. 'Oh dear, you too?' He lowered his voice to a blood-curdling whisper. 'Then tread softly gentlemen, or I'll turn you all into toads!' He heard the faintest of sounds behind him as Leela slipped away into the undergrowth.

As the Doctor came up to the nearest warrior, the man cowered back, again touching throat, shoulder and hip in the sign of protection. 'That gesture you all make,' said the Doctor conversationally. 'Presumably it's to ward off evil? But do you realise it's also the sequence for checking the seals on a Starfall Seven space suit? And what makes it especially interesting is that none of you know what a space suit is—do you?'

The Doctor snatched a jelly baby from the bag in his pocket and held it under the astonished warrior's nose. 'Now drop your weapons all of you—or I'll kill your friend here with this deadly jelly baby!'

But the warriors ignored the threat, levelling their crossbows at the Doctor. 'Kill him, then,' challenged the leader. The Doctor paused. Leela should be well clear by now. He popped the jelly baby into his mouth and said rather indistinctly, 'I don't take orders from you, my good man. Take me to your leader.'

It was late by the time the Doctor and his guards reached the village. They had taken him a long, roundabout way through the forest, and during the last stages of the journey they had insisted on blindfolding him with his own scarf. The Doctor had submitted without resistance. He was determined to find out what was going on on this strange planet, and the village seemed as good a place to start as any.

He knew when they'd arrived by the harsh challenge of the sentry at the gate, the muttered replies of his guards. He was bustled into some kind of building. 'Bring it forward,' commanded a gruff voice, and the scarf was roughly pulled from the Doctor's eyes.

He found himself in the middle of a huge circular hut lit by flaring torches set around the walls. Immediately before him was a metal chair upon which sat a grizzled warrior in ornate ceremonial robes. (The

29

Doctor noticed without much surprise that the metal throne was the ejector seat of a Starfall Seven space ship, and the Chief's regalia included a space-sextant slung round his neck on a leather thong.) The hut was full of savage-looking skin-clad warriors, armed with crossbows, spears and knives.

As the scarf fell away and the Doctor's face was revealed, there was a gasp of horror. Undaunted by this reception, he said cheerfully, 'Good evening. I think you're all going to be very happy I came here tonight.'

In the rear wall of the Sanctum the point of a knife suddenly appeared through the woven reeds of the wall. The knife point was pulled back, leaving a small hole in the wall. From the other side, Leela peered through it—just in time to see Neeva adjust his ceremonial robes and sweep out into the main hut. Despite her suspicions of the Doctor she found she was unable to leave him to his fate. Quickly she set to work to enlarge the hole.

The Doctor stood very still as the fantastic figure strode towards him. But now his calm was shaken at the sight of the complex arrangement of transparent tubing and electronic circuitry that the Witch Doctor was brandishing under his nose.

'I should be careful with that thing if I were you ... It's an ultrabeam accelerator.'

Neeva sneered. 'See how *it* fears the sacred relics of Xoanon!'

'There happens to be a charge in there, you could

transform this whole village into a smoky hole in the ground.'

'Hear how *it* threatens us!' chanted Neeva.

'Why don't you just untie my hands,' suggested the Doctor. 'I've an idea what happened here. Perhaps I can help to solve your problems.'

'Hear how *it* squirms for release!' gloated Neeva. '*It* cannot deceive us.'

The Doctor sighed. 'No, I can see you're a figure of superior intellect. You're Neeva, I take it?' He looked up at the figure on the throne. 'Are you the leader of this Tribe—or is he?'

Andor came down from his throne. 'Bring *it* closer,' he ordered. Guards thrust the Doctor forward, and Andor glared threateningly into his face. 'Speak, Evil One. Will you release our god Xoanon?'

'Gladly, if I was holding him prisoner. But I'm not.' There was an angry muttering from the warriors.

Andor's hand went to the knife in his belt. 'Then you must be destroyed, so that *we* may release him.' Knife in hand, he advanced upon the Doctor.

4

The Face on the Mountain

Leela squeezed through the hole in the wall and moved over to the door of the Sanctum. She looked out into the Council hut—saw Andor advancing menacingly on the Doctor and drew her own knife. She was about to make a desperate attempt at rescue when she heard Neeva's voice. 'Wait, Andor. I will speak the Litany before the warriors. Then the Evil One shall be sacrificed before them, and they will know that victory will be ours.'

'Very well.'

Neeva turned away. 'I shall return to the Sanctum and prepare myself.'

Andor turned to his chief guard. 'Give the signal to summon the rest of the Tribe, the rest of you, assemble them outside.' The guards hurried away.

'Don't hurry on my account,' called the Doctor. No one took any notice.

The chief guard made his way to the centre of the village where a huge metal panel hung suspended from a wooden frame. Picking up the metal rod which hung nearby, the guard began beating on the panel, summoning the full Tribe to assemble before the Council hut. The gong was a sacred relic of the Old Time, and the faded lettering stamped along the bottom edge formed the words, 'Survey Team 6'. But no one in the Tribe of Sevateem could read.

Only the Doctor, Andor and a solitary guard were left in the Council hut now. Neeva was at prayer in his Sanctum and the others had gone to assemble the people. The Doctor heard the murmur of a steadily growing crowd outside the hut. Clearly his execution was to be something of a public event. He used the brief respite to try to talk to the Chief. 'Andor, will you listen to me! I am not the Evil One. I'm a traveller, that's all. Your tribe has obviously been visited by travellers before.'

Andor backed away, as if the Doctor's words were some terrible blasphemy. 'That's impossible.'

'Space travellers, Andor, men from some other world. This place is littered with their equipment, the remains of their weapons and tools. Your legend of a captive god is obviously related to them in some way.'

Andor turned to the warrior. 'Guard *it* well. Do not listen to *its* words, they are evil and will corrupt you.' He turned and strode away.

'Andor, wait,' called the Doctor. 'Killing me isn't going to help you!' As the Chief hurried from the Council hut the Doctor added mournfully, 'And it's not going to do me much good either, is it?'

The guard stared impassively at the Doctor, tightening his grip on his crossbow.

Neeva knelt before the altar, chanting his prayers. 'And let the Tribe of Sevateem partake of your strength oh Xoanon, so that they may at last inherit thy kingdom. Hear thy servant Neeva, Shaman of the Sevateem. Hear me, Xoanon, hear my prayer!'

Leela crouched low behind the altar. She had ducked behind it for cover when Neeva re-entered the Sanctum, and had been there ever since, motionless as a statue. Despite the ache in her muscles she dared not make the slightest movement.

Neeva finished his prayers at last, made a final bow to the altar and left the Sanctum. Leela emerged from hiding and crept to the doorway. She saw the Doctor waiting alone before the empty throne, and heard Neeva's low-voiced conversation with the guard. 'When I reach the end of the Litany—bring *it* forth. You know what to do then?'

The guard nodded, his eyes on the Doctor.

Neeva went over to the entrance of the Council hut.

Leela could see the Doctor's fingers hard at work on the thongs that bound his wrists behind his back. He didn't seem to be getting anywhere. The guard came forward suspiciously and the Doctor beamed innocently at him.

The open space outside the Council hut was packed. Everyone in the Tribe was there, drawn by the astonishing rumour that the Evil One had been captured, and was to be sacrificed to ensure victory. Neeva

34

raised his arms and the excited crowd became completely silent. He began to chant the Litany and the crowd made their familiar responses, quietly at first then with increasing fervour.

'Our fathers of the Tribe of Sevateem were sent forth by our god to seek Paradise,' chanted Neeva.

'And still we seek,' chanted the crowd.

'They searched and found it not, but while they searched, the Tribe of Tesh who remained at the Place of Land betrayed our fathers.'

'Death to the traitor Tesh.'

Inside the hut the Doctor was listening intently to Neeva's words. Here in this strange, confused Litany was the history of his captors, changed and garbled over generation after generation.

Neeva's voice came clearly from outside the hut. 'The Tesh made a pact with the Evil One and our god turned his face from us. The Evil One raised the Tower and defended it with the Black Wall, to aid the Tribe of Tesh.'

The Doctor and the guard were both intent on the Litany, though for very different reasons. Neither noticed Leela's silent approach. Suddenly she sprang forward, and slapped the guard on the back of his neck with the palm of her hand.

The guard stood quite still, staring ahead with bulging eyes, then pitched forward on to his face.

The Doctor turned, saw the fallen body, and Leela's exultant grin. 'How did you do that?'

Leela held out her hand, palm upwards. The point

35

of a large thorn projected from between her fingers. 'Janis thorn. It paralyses instantly and death follows soon afterwards. There's no cure.'

The Doctor glared at her and Leela realised with some surprise that he was angry about the death of the guard. 'It was necessary,' she explained. 'Come on.'

The chanting of the crowd outside grew louder and fiercer. '*Cursed be the Tribe of Tesh. Cursed be the Tribe of Tesh.*' Then Neeva's voice again. 'And the Tribe of Tesh stand between the Tribe of Sevateem and Xoanon, god of their fathers. We must kill the servants of the Evil One.'

The voice of the crowd was a maddened roar. '*Kill the Tesh. Kill the Tesh. Kill the Tesh!*'

Leela tried to pull the Doctor away but he resisted. 'No, Leela I want to listen.'

'We haven't time to listen. He's coming to the bit about destroying the Evil One. That's supposed to be you, remember?'

'You know this Litany, Leela?'

'Of course I do, we're taught it as children.'

'Good,' said the Doctor briskly. 'Come on then, don't dawdle.'

Leela led him into the Sanctum and across to the gap in the wall. From outside they could still hear Neeva's voice. 'Now is the time when the Sevateem shall rise in their wrath and kill the Evil One.'

'*Destroy it. Destroy it. Destroy it.*'

After this resounding climax there came a silence, caused, the Doctor guessed, by his failure to appear on cue and take the leading role. Leela was already through the gap, and the Doctor began struggling after her.

A guard rushed into the Council hut, looked round and found it empty, except for the huddled body. '*It* has escaped,' he bellowed. 'The Evil One has escaped!'

The Doctor got stuck halfway and struggled desperately to enlarge the hole.

Neeva ran into the Council hut, more guards behind him. 'Find *it*,' he screamed. 'Find *it*! Search everywhere!'

The guards began running aimlessly about the hut, but one, brighter than the rest, headed for the doorway of the Sanctum. He pulled back the curtain and saw the Doctor struggling to get through the hole. '*It*'s here,' he yelled, and rushed forward, spear raised.

With a final desperate heave the Doctor shot through the hole.

The guard dived after him—and as his head and shoulders appeared, Leela slapped him on the neck with another Janis thorn. The guard stiffened and then slumped. Leela grabbed the body and heaved it forward, spreading the arms wide so it couldn't be pulled back. 'Just covering our retreat,' she explained.

'That wasn't necessary, Leela,' said the Doctor angrily. 'Who gave you licence to slaughter? No more Janis thorns, you understand—ever.'

Leela gave him a puzzled look, and they set off at a run. Since everyone in the village was milling about in front of the Council hut, they made their way through the empty village unobserved. Soon they were hurrying through the dark forest.

Outside the Council hut, Andor had been told what had happened. '*It* must be recaptured,' he ordered.

'It is imperative. Tomas, take four good men and search beyond the village.'

Tomas said, 'Right, Andor,' and began selecting his men from the crowd.

'Quickly, Tomas,' urged Calib. He himself went through the Council hut and into the Sanctum.

Neeva looked up from his prayers before the altar. 'Well, Calib. Has *it* been re-captured?'

'*It* got away.'

'*It* must be captured and destroyed.'

'Andor has sent Tomas with a search party. If they fail, he will send others.'

'Too late,' said Neeva impatiently. 'Whatever happens, the attack on the Wall must not be delayed.'

Leela moved swiftly through the forest, the Doctor close behind her. 'We've lost them,' gasped Leela. 'We'll come to the edge of the forest soon. We can rest there.'

They moved on a little more slowly now, and soon the trees began to thin out. At last they came to the forest edge. It was nearly dawn and the Doctor saw they were on a kind of plateau, looking across a little valley. On the far side rose the towering shape of a mountain. The Doctor looked across at it, casually at first, then with increasing fascination. The mountain seemed to have a kind of shape to it ... 'What is it, Leela?'

'That's the Evil One.'

As it grew lighter, the Doctor could see that a jutting spur of the mountain had been carved into an enormous face. It stared arrogantly across the valley at him. The Doctor shook his head in astonishment. 'It seems I *have* been here before. I must have made quite an impression.'

The face carved into the mountain was his own.

5

Attack

The Doctor stared across the valley. He had never been particularly modest, but there was something rather embarrassing at seeing one's own colossally magnified features carved onto a mountain. 'Who put it there?' he asked. 'How was it done?'

Leela shrugged. 'The Tesh did it with their magic. They set the Face of Evil on the mountain to taunt us.'

The Doctor nodded. Presumably the face had been carved out of the mountain with a laser-beam. Either that, or a few hundred years' work with hammer and chisels.

Leela looked across at the mountain, then back at the Doctor. 'What happened when you were here before?' she asked. 'You must be able to remember!'

'Of course I can,' said the Doctor defensively. He hesitated. 'Well, I'm trying to. One or two details are still eluding me. Perhaps I was on some other part of the planet.'

'There is no other part. Only beyond the Wall.'

'Beyond the Wall? I wonder ...' The Doctor stood gazing across the valley, lost in thought.

'Wonder what?'

'Sssh! I'm wondering.' He came to a decision. 'Back to the village, I think. Maybe some of those "sacred relics" of Neeva's will jog my memory.'

Leela was horrified. 'We can't go back, Doctor. We'll be torn to pieces.'

'Only if they catch us,' said the Doctor cheerfully. 'Besides, they'll be too busy getting ready for their attack to bother with us.'

'That's what you said last time—remember?'

The Doctor chuckled. 'You mustn't expect perfection, Leela—even from me!'

Andor glared angrily at his Witch Doctor. 'I tell you the men are afraid to attack while the Evil One is still out there.'

Neeva looked up at the Chief, running a hand over his shaven head. 'I have been thinking,' he said cunningly. 'If we tell them *it* has been destroyed ...'

'No! I will not lie to my people.'

'Soon the Wall will open,' insisted Neeva. 'We know that it stays open for a very short time. We dare not delay. Attack now, or we betray our god.'

Andor tugged his beard. 'Has Xoanon commanded this?'

'He has.' There was utter certainty in Neeva's voice.

Andor called to the guard at the door of the Council hut. 'Guard. Sound the summons to attack.' As the guard ran out, Andor rose from his throne. 'You'd better be right, Neeva. Servant of Xoanon or not, if we fail—I'll kill you!'

Neeva did not flinch. 'Xoanon has promised us victory.'

'No,' said Andor heavily. 'He has promised you—

and you have promised us. You will tell the warriors that *it* was captured and killed in the forest.'

The clamour of the signal gong began resounding through the village.

Arguing furiously, the Doctor and Leela crouched in the woods outside the village. Leela was trying to persuade the Doctor to abandon his plans. 'Returning to the village is dangerous enough. But the shrine of Xoanon ...'

'I must examine those relics. And listen, isn't that the signal gong?'

Leela nodded reluctantly. 'They must be preparing to leave for the attack on the Wall. They will gather in the square before the Council hut.'

'Now's our chance then. Come on.' The Doctor set off for the scattered huts at the back of the village.

To Leela's surprise they actually managed to reach the rear wall of the Sanctum without being seen. The hole they'd escaped through had been hastily patched up and there was a large gap at the edge. Holding up his hand for silence, the Doctor listened at the gap, and Leela did the same. From the Sanctum came the low mumble of Neeva's voice. 'Oh great god Xoanon, speak that I may know thy will.'

They peered through the hole. Neeva was still kneeling before the altar. 'Speak, Xoanon, speak!' Neeva paused, and seemed to be waiting expectantly.

A guard appeared in the doorway. 'Shaman Neeva, it is time to leave.'

'I am coming.'

'Chief Andor asked that you do not delay.'

'I said I'm coming!' The frightened guard fled. Neeva waited a moment longer, then got reluctantly to his feet. He took off his space-suit cloak and arranged it on a special stand. From another stand he took a different cloak, this one made from lengths of plastic tubing and strips of electric cable. He placed a glove-like hat on his head and left the Sanctum.

The Doctor and Leela had watched all this through the gap. 'I like the hat,' whispered the Doctor. 'Very fetching.'

'That is the Hand of Xoanon,' said Leela reprovingly.

'That is an armoured space-glove, or what's left of one.' The Doctor started wrenching the repair-patch from the hole.

Outside the Council hut, the warriors were gathering. Their mood was sullen and rebellious, and Andor and Neeva were doing their best to whip them into a state of enthusiasm. 'The attack must begin at once,' roared Andor.

Neeva joined in. 'Soon the Wall will open. Xoanon has spoken. Now that the Evil One is dead, we cannot fail!' He began to chant the Litany. Reluctantly at first, then with increasing fervour, the warriors gave their responses. Soon the familiar ritual had them in its spell and their eyes blazed with anger as they shouted their hatred of the Tesh.

The Doctor ripped aside the last of the matting and squeezed through the hole. Leela followed him. Once inside the Sanctum the Doctor headed straight for the altar. He began to examine the sacred relics of Xoanon, handling them with a familiarity which made Leela shudder.

The Doctor looked up and said thoughtfully, 'You know, I had the distinct feeling that Neeva expected an answer to that prayer of his.'

'Wouldn't be much point in praying if he didn't.'

The Doctor smiled. 'I've met theologians who'd give you an argument on that. No, I mean he was listening.'

The Doctor picked up a plastic tube packed with complex circuits and pressed a switch in its side. 'Hello, transgalactic operator, hello!' He listened for a moment then tossed the tube aside. 'Nothing. Dead as a Dalek.'

Leela stared at him. 'Why did you speak to that tube?'

'I thought I recognised it.' The Doctor was gazing abstractedly round the Sanctum and his eyes fell on the space-suit cloak on its stand. He crossed over to it and began fiddling with the controls set inside the helmet.

A voice from inside the helmet said, 'Neeva! Neeva, is that you?'

Leela was terrified. She dropped to her knees, making the sign of protection.

The Doctor was almost equally surprised. Not just because of the voice—he'd been hoping for a reply from the transceiver inside the helmet. What astoni-

44

shed the Doctor was the fact that the voice he heard was his own!

'A hot line to god,' he murmured. 'Lucky old Neeva.' He looked down at Leela. 'Don't be afraid, it's only a machine for sending voices over long distances. If that *is* Xoanon speaking, then he isn't a god. Gods don't need to use machines.'

Still a little fearful, Leela straightened up. 'Are you certain?'

'Of course I am. Aren't you?'

'Yes,' said Leela hesitantly. 'Yes, I suppose so.'

'That's better.'

The voice spoke again. 'Neeva! Neeva!'

The Doctor said politely, 'I'm sorry, Neeva isn't here at the moment. Can I take a message?'

There was a long silence. Then the voice chanted, 'At last we are here. At last. At last. Us!'

'Us?'

'You. Me. Us,' crooned the voice. 'At last I shall be free of us.'

'Who are you?' demanded the Doctor.

The voice was surprised. 'Don't I know?' The transceiver clicked off, and there was silence.

Leela looked at the Doctor. He was standing like someone in a trance, staring wide-eyed into the distance. 'Leela, I'm beginning to get a very nasty idea ...'

'What idea?'

The Doctor seemed to be talking to himself. 'Something *I* did? It seems like it ...'

'What are you talking about?'

'Who did that voice remind you of?'

'You? Yes that's it, it was your voice. How could that be?'

'More to the point, who could that be? I think it's time I took a look at this Wall of yours.'

Andor was leading the warriors of the Sevateem along the forest path that led to the Wall. Beside him marched Neeva in his Shaman's robe. Andor glanced over his shoulder at the file of warriors behind him. A pitiful handful they were too, he thought. The Sevateem were dwindling year by year. Hunting accidents, famine, disease, and above all the endless futile attacks upon the Wall had reduced their numbers to a few grizzled warriors together with the boys who had just attained manhood. Much more of this and Xoanon would have no Sevateem left to worship him. Still, this time it was going to be different. This time they were going to storm the Wall, rescue Xoanon, and bring about an age of endless peace and prosperity for the tribe. Andor was doing his best to make himself believe that Neeva's prophecies would all come true. But his heart was full of dread as he led his men along the trail.

Tomas appeared ahead, running back towards them. 'I saw the Wall,' he gasped, as he came up to them.

Andor gripped his arm. 'Was there a gap?'

Tomas nodded. 'It is as Neeva prophesied! The gap is there! It's like before—a sort of shining tunnel.'

'How wide?'

'Big enough for three men, perhaps four.'

Andor tugged his beard. 'I still don't like it.'

'You think it's a trap?'

Neeva came forward. 'Xoanon is fighting on our side. Even though he is held captive, he has summoned all his power to make the gap, so that we may rescue him. Unless we attack *now* his powers will fade and the gap will close. Xoanon would not lay traps for his people.'

'The Tesh might,' said Andor stubbornly. 'Or the Evil One.'

Tomas looked at him in surprise. 'Neeva told us that the Evil One has been destroyed.'

Andor glanced quickly at Neeva. 'Yes, that's true. So *it* has.' He came to his decision. 'Come, we've wasted enough time. I'll lead the main attack. You take the left flank, Tomas, Calib the right.' Andor raised his hand and the little column began to move forward.

In a distant part of the forest, the Doctor had reached another part of the Wall. He stood gazing thoughtfully up at it, Leela by his side. It was an astonishing sight, a sheet of pure true blackness, a nothingness, stretching in all directions. To the left, to the right, and high above them there was the same dead blackness. The forest seemed to border it on either side.

'It's a Time Barrier,' said the Doctor softly.

'I don't understand.'

'The principle's very simple. You just move everything inside the barrier forward a couple of seconds. The result is your Wall—a barrier completely impervious to all forms of energy. I've seen it done as a

47

parlour trick, but never on this scale.'

'Is there any way to get past it?'

'Only one. It can be bridged from within, by whoever set it up.'

Leela told him of the gaps that appeared in the Wall from time to time, of the always-futile attacks made by the Sevateem in their attempts to rescue the captive god Xoanon. 'Andor and the others are about to attack again at some other part of the Wall. But if what you say is true, they're walking into a trap. Can't we warn them?'

'Too late,' said the Doctor sadly. 'The attack will be starting at any moment. Anyway, they wouldn't listen.'

'Calib might. He's more intelligent than the others —more open-minded. Come on, Doctor. Let's try.' She looked pleadingly at him, and after a moment the Doctor nodded. They turned away from the blackness of the Wall and headed back to the village.

Andor and his warriors crouched at the edge of the forest. Just as Tomas had reported, a kind of radiant tunnel had appeared in the blackness of the Wall. It stretched temptingly ahead of them. The gateway to Paradise.

Andor drew a deep breath then rose to his feet. 'Attack!' he yelled. 'Come on all of you. Attack!'

Warriors at his heels, Andor dashed forward. There was no planning, no strategy, just a headlong charge. As the Sevateem followed their Chief into the tunnel, Neeva stood at the edge of the forest, arms held high in prayer. 'Protect your warriors, oh Xoanon. Strengthen their arms so that at last they may free you.'

Suddenly a fierce white light blazed from the mouth of the tunnel, swallowing up Andor and his warriors. Yelling and screaming they disappeared into its radiance, brandishing spears and firing crossbows.

Tomas turned to his men. 'Attack!' he yelled, and led his warriors in a charge. 'Come on, Calib.'

As Tomas and his warriors dashed into the blinding radiance, Calib's men looked fearfully at him. Calib stood watching silently. He made no attempt to lead his men to the attack.

A high-pitched electronic howl filled the air, and all round the tunnel men twisted and fell. Soon the air was filled with the screams of the dying. The tunnel began to close . . .

6

Danger for Leela

Hands plunged deep into his pockets the Doctor stood waiting in the middle of the empty Council hut. Leela was by the entrance, keeping watch. A solitary figure appeared and she ducked back out of sight. 'He's coming, Doctor,' she hissed. 'I told you Calib would survive if anyone did.'

Calib came wearily into the hut—and stopped in astonishment at the sight of the Doctor.

The Doctor beamed. 'Ah, there you are, Calib. I was just thinking about you.'

Calib stood warily, crossbow in hand. 'So Neeva and Andor lied to us.'

'I wouldn't be surprised. By the way Leela's just behind you.'

Calib whirled round. Leela was by the doorway covering him with her crossbow. 'Ah,' he said thoughtfully, and stood very still. Leela made an impatient gesture and Calib put down his crossbow on a nearby bench.

'How was your battle?' asked the Doctor.

'Like the last time.'

Leela looked at him in anguish. 'Another massacre?'

Calib nodded wearily. 'There was this blinding light, and a terrible noise. Then the Wall closed up.

We never even saw the Tesh, and more than half the men were killed.'

'But not you,' said Leela flatly. 'You seem unhurt.'

Calib shrugged. 'There's no particular virtue in dying, Leela.'

Leela's voice was scornful. 'That depends on what you do to avoid it.'

'Now, Leela,' said the Doctor. 'Let's not quarrel. I'm sure Calib is a reasonable man. After all, we came here to talk to him.'

'What do you want of me, Doctor?' asked Calib curiously.

'We need someone's help—and Leela thinks it might be yours.'

Calib looked distrustfully at Leela. 'Why me?'

Leela moved closer to him. 'The Tribe is in desperate danger, Calib,' she said urgently. 'The Doctor is the only one who can help us. We've got to convince the others he's not the Evil One.'

'Having convinced you first, of course,' added the Doctor.

'I don't think you're the Evil One—I never have. I don't believe in evil spirits.'

'I'm impressed,' said the Doctor. 'It looks as though Leela was right about you.'

Calib strolled closer to Leela, ignoring the threatening crossbow. 'If I'm to help you, I'll need to know everything you've discovered.'

The Doctor frowned. 'Well, there isn't much time ... Leela showed me this Wall of yours, and in my opinion ...'

Calib's hand flashed out and Leela staggered back.

Calib snatched the crossbow from her weakening grasp. As she fell, Leela stretched out a hand to the Doctor, as if in appeal. An ugly black shape was embedded in the back.

'What have you done to her?' shouted the Doctor.

'Janis thorn. Something you hadn't thought of, Doctor.'

The Doctor started moving towards Leela. Calib made a threatening gesture with the bow. 'Stay where you are!'

'I thought you were being convinced a bit too easily.'

'Oh, I meant what I said, Doctor. I don't believe you're the Evil One—but the others do. Neeva said you'd been destroyed, and here you are. Just the evidence I need to break him.'

'Leela underestimated your ambition,' said the Doctor softly.

'It's for the good of the Tribe.'

The Doctor looked down at Leela. 'Naturally. And this too?'

'She might have tried to stop me,' said Calib simply. 'I said stay where you are!'

'You need me alive—remember?' The Doctor knelt beside Leela and began feeling her wrist for a pulse.

'Calib, you held back! You cost us the attack!'

Calib turned. Tomas stood in the doorway, battle-stained, weary, and very angry.

Suddenly the Doctor threw himself backwards and swung his legs round in a sweeping arc, that knocked Calib's legs from under him. Calib tried to get up but the Doctor was already on his feet. Snatching the crossbow from Calib's hands he stood towering over him, and spoke without looking round. 'Come in, whoever you are. Who are you by the way?'

'Tomas. What's happened to Leela?'

'Calib here poisoned her with a Janis thorn. Up you get, Calib.'

'I think you've broken my leg.'

'I'll break your nose if you don't get up,' said the Doctor savagely.

Calib struggled to his feet, looking at the Doctor's crossbow. 'It takes skill to use one of those things.'

'What, at this range? All it takes is a flick of the wrist. Now, pick Leela up and carry her in there.' The Doctor nodded towards Neeva's Sanctum. 'Tomas, you help him.'

Tomas and Calib carried Leela into the Sanctum and the Doctor pointed towards a low bed in one corner. 'Put her on there. Gently, now.'

They lowered Leela on to the bed. 'What are you going to do?' asked Calib.

The Doctor looked at Tomas. 'Tomas, you don't want her to die, do you?'

'Of course not.'

'Then keep him covered for me. I need time to work.'

The Doctor passed the crossbow to Tomas, and began examining the sacred relics on the altar.

Tomas looked a little bemusedly at the bow in his hands and Calib took a step towards the door. Tomas raised the bow to cover him. 'I wouldn't do that, Calib.'

'Don't be a fool, Tomas, I'm going to give the alarm.'

'Back against the wall!'

Calib looked hard at him, realised he wasn't bluffing, and moved away from the door.

Tomas shot a quick glance at the Doctor, who was still rummaging ruthlessly through the sacred relics. 'What are you doing, Doctor?'

'Ah, here we are.' The Doctor looked up. 'This is a space-ship's medikit, Tomas, and this is a bio-analyser. If I can identify the poison, I can programme the medikit to make an anti-toxin.'

The medikit was a small oblong box with a row of lights and a control keyboard set into the lid. Tomas watched as the Doctor removed a strip of clear plastic from a holder at the back, plucked the Janis thorn from the back of Leela's hand, and rubbed the poisonous tip of the thorn on to the strip. He fed the strip into a slot in the side of the machine. There was a whirring sound and the lights on the medikit began flashing in a complicated sequence. The Doctor studied them for a moment, took a second poison-smear from the thorn, feeding this one into the slide-tray of the bio-analyser, a kind of miniature electron microscope. He peered into the eye-piece for a moment, gave a grunt of satisfaction, went back to the medikit and punched out a complicated series of numbers on the keyboard.

Lights began flashing on, and soon the lights on the display panel were burning steadily. All except one, which was still flashing. The Doctor studied the keyboard for a moment, then punched in more instructions. The light flashed for a moment longer, then burned steadily like the others. 'Got it,' said the

Doctor triumphantly. The little machine began a satisfied whirring. 'Well, come on, come on,' said the Doctor impatiently.

Calib said mockingly, 'What do you suppose he's doing, Tomas? You don't really believe he can help Leela by poking around in Neeva's relics!'

The Doctor kept his eye on the machine. 'Shut up, rattlesnake,' he said abstractedly. 'I'm trying to save time. Leela hasn't much left.'

Tomas looked down at Leela. She lay perfectly still, eyes wide open and staring. 'I think it's too late, Doctor. She's already dead.'

The medikit gave a sudden triumphant buzz and a little tray popped out of its side. In the tray lay a small plastic syringe.

The Doctor snatched it up, crossed to Leela and injected the anti-toxin into her arm. For a moment nothing happened. Seeing that the Doctor and Tomas had their eyes fixed on Leela, Calib began sidling toward the door. The Doctor leaned over Leela and slapped her hard. She twitched and stirred. Then she blinked, and her eyes began to focus. 'Doctor?' she said dazedly.

Suddenly Tomas realised. 'Calib's gone. He must have slipped out while——'

'Watch the door,' ordered the Doctor. He helped Leela to sit up. 'Are you all right?'

'I seem to be. I ought to be dead, though. There's no cure for the Janis thorn.'

'Oh yes there is. Just a question of finding it.'

'Do you know the answer to everything?'

'Of course,' said the Doctor. 'Answers are easy.

55

Asking the right questions is the tricky part.'

From the doorway Tomas called, 'They're coming, Doctor.'

The Doctor looked at Leela. 'Can you walk?'

'I think so. My arm hurts a bit.'

'That'll wear off. Tomas, you take Leela out the back way.' He pointed to the hole in the wall.

'I'm staying with you,' said Leela firmly.

'You're going with Tomas,' said the Doctor, even more firmly. 'I'll see you both later.'

Before they could argue, he strolled calmly through into the Council hut.

Since the Doctor's capture was now inevitable, Tomas saw no reason to delay. He grabbed Leela and dragged her towards the hole.

As the Doctor came out of the Sanctum, Calib ran in, guards behind him. 'Good evening, gentlemen,' said the Doctor breezily. 'I thought you'd never get here. Good Heavens, look at that!' His eyes widened and he stared over their shoulders.

It was the oldest trick in the world, but Calib and the others fell for it. They whirled round. By the time they had realised there was nothing behind them and turned back, the Doctor appeared to have vanished.

'Over here, gentlemen,' said a cheerful voice from above them. They looked up. The Doctor was sprawled comfortably on the Chief's throne. 'Now then, shall we get down to business?'

The guards ran to the throne and surrounded it, covering the Doctor with their crossbows. He looked round at the circle of fierce, unfriendly faces. 'You know, I shall begin to think you don't like me!'

56

Neeva hurried into the Council hut, pushed through the ring of guards and stared malevolently at the Doctor.

The Doctor smiled. 'Ah, Neeva, is it really you? They told me you were dead. Or was it the other way round?'

Tomas squeezed through the hole and turned to help Leela. As she emerged and straightened up, warriors came out of the forest and surrounded them.

Andor limped forward. 'Neeva was right. You're both in league with the Evil One.'

'You blind fool,' began Tomas. Andor turned away.

'Seize them,' he ordered.

The warriors closed in.

7

The Test of the Horda

It was becoming quite a lively debate, thought the
Doctor. The Council hut was packed with the sur-
vivors of the raid, and everyone else in the village
who could squeeze in. Andor was presiding from his
throne, Neeva and Calib beside him. The Doctor,
Leela and Tomas stood before the throne. All three
had their hands bound in front of them with leather
thongs.

A grizzled old warrior had stepped out of the crowd
to challenge Neeva. 'You lied to us,' he accused. 'You
said *it* was destroyed.'

An angry roar from the crowd showed how many of
the warriors supported him.

Calib said smoothly, 'Answer them, Neeva. Tell
them what happened.'

Neeva held up his hands for silence. 'Did *it* not
bring the witch its servant back to life? I tell you *it*
was destroyed—but *it* renewed itself.'

The Doctor decided to join in. 'If you believe that,
you'll believe anything. Leela isn't a witch—and I'm
not the Evil One.'

'You wiped out our attack,' charged Andor.

'Piffle. I was nowhere near.'

'That's true,' shouted Leela. 'I was with him all the
time.'

Neeva turned angrily on her. 'Ha! Will you believe the words of this witch?'

The Doctor said calmly, 'The attack failed because it was a trap, right from the start.'

'And who could have laid such a trap?' sneered Neeva.

Leela's voice rang through the Council hut. 'Xoanon!' There was a moment of appalled silence, then a roar of fury from the crowd. They surged forward menacingly, and Andor's guards actually had to raise their spears to hold them back. Leela heard Tomas whispering in her ear, 'A great mistake, saying that!' Listening to the angry crowd Leela felt he might well be right.

'They must all be destroyed,' screamed Neeva. 'Totally destroyed this time. Throw them to the Horda.'

'What *is* a Horda anyway,' asked the Doctor plaintively, but no one answered. Leela shuddered.

Calib was addressing the crowd. 'Wait! I do not believe this *is* the Evil One.'

There was a mutter of astonishment from the crowd. Leela edged closer to the Doctor. 'Conscience?'

'No, politics. Calib wants to break Neeva's hold on the Tribe. If he can prove Neeva wrong about a religious matter like this . . .'

'Listen to me,' shouted Calib. 'If he can be killed, then he's not the Evil One—because the Evil One is a god.'

'Good point,' said the Doctor appreciatively. 'Fifteen love.' Leela looked blankly at him. The ancient Earth game of tennis meant nothing to her.

Neeva pointed dramatically at the Doctor. 'The

Litany says *it* can be destroyed.'

The Doctor was still keeping score. 'Fifteen all!'

Calib glared challengingly at Neeva. 'I say we should put this Doctor to the Test and see if he speaks truly.'

Andor intervened. 'The Test is for mortals.'

'If he can be killed, then he is a mortal.'

The Doctor chuckled. 'Game, set and match to Calib, I think!'

Leela looked wonderingly at him. How could he be so cheerful when he'd just been condemned to an agonising death?

The Pit of the Horda was in a screened enclosure on the outskirts of the village. It was a sacred place, a place of terror. It was the Place of the Ordeal.

The pit was very large, oblong in shape, covered by two stone shutters. In the centre of the shutters, at right angles to the line where they met, was carved a long shallow trough.

The area around the pit was enclosed with wattle screens. In one of them was a small window-like opening. Through it could be seen an enormous rock, suspended high in the air from a rope, which ran up to a huge wooden derrick. Beside the pit itself was a large lever in a wooden framework. Taut ropes ran from the lever and disappeared behind the screen.

The Doctor stood by the pit, looking keenly around him, trying to work out the meaning of this strange and complicated set-up. Presumably the hanging rock was a counter-balance, to open the shutters... Leela and Tomas were beside him. Their hands were still bound, though the Doctor's had been freed in preparation for the Ordeal.

Calib and Andor were there too, and a small group of Tribal Councillors and guards. Only Neeva was absent. On his defeat by Calib, he had stalked into the Sanctum in a huff, presumably to take counsel with Xoanon.

The Doctor looked around the assembled audience. 'Well, let's get on with it, gentlemen.'

At a nod from Calib, who seemed to be in charge of the proceedings, a guard came forward with a wicker basket. He tipped the contents onto the ground and jumped back hurriedly. The Doctor looked down. There at his feet was a white, snake-like creature, rather like a giant slow-worm. It was wriggling lethargically. 'So that's a Horda. Doesn't look too formidable. What am I supposed to do, fight it or eat it?'

Calib took a spear from a guard and poked at the Horda with the butt. The creature reared up and struck at the spear-haft with incredible speed, locking onto the wood with rows of savage teeth.

Calib held up the spear. The Horda hung for a moment by its teeth, then realising that the wood wasn't good to eat, released its hold and dropped to the ground and lay quiet.

'They'll strike at anything that moves except each other,' said Calib. 'Ten of them can strip the flesh from a man's bones before he can cry out.'

'And I take it there are rather more than ten of them in there?'

'The pit is full of them,' said Calib. He nodded to

a guard who came forward with a long narrow plank. He laid it in the trough across the shutters. It fitted exactly.

'You stand on that,' explained Calib.

'And then what?'

Calib pointed to the suspended boulder. 'The stone is lowered, the shutters begin to open, the plank becomes a bridge.'

'And what do I do?'

'To survive, you must break the rope—with this!'

Calib took a loaded crossbow from the nearest guard and handed it to the Doctor.

The Doctor took the crossbow, and immediately the surrounding guards trained their own weapons upon him. He weighed the crossbow in his hands, looking at the pit, the plank, and the hanging boulder.

'Doctor listen,' said Leela urgently. 'The rope gets thinner the further it goes down, but it moves faster too!'

One of the guards struck her savagely across the face. 'Silence, witch! He does it alone.'

'Who is that man?' asked the Doctor mildly.

Calib stared at him. 'Which man?'

'That one,' snapped the Doctor. Snatching the spear from Calib's hand he used it to flick the Horda at the guard. It fastened itself to the man's clothes and he fled screaming through the crowd. 'Whoops, sorry,' said the Doctor apologetically. He strolled to the centre of the plank and stood waiting. 'Well?'

Andor raised his hand. 'Let the Test of the Horda begin.'

A guard pulled a lever and the massive boulder

began its slow descent. Soon it disappeared from sight behind the screen.

Slowly the stone shutters began to draw apart. The plank became a bridge—but a bridge over a steadily increasing gap. As the gap widened a whispering, rustling, hissing noise could be heard—the sound of many living creatures in constant motion. The Doctor glanced down. The pit below him was filled with a seething mass of Horda.

As the gap beneath the plank became wider and wider, the plank began to sag and creak. The Doctor realised that if the gap became too wide the plank would snap beneath his weight.

It was an interesting problem, he thought. If he fired too soon, the rope would still be too thick to be broken by the crossbow bolt. If he left it too late, the plank would snap and he would fall into the pit. The Doctor looked through the screen window at the rope. As Leela had warned him, it was getting steadily thinner, but it was moving fast too ... Just a little longer ...

The sight of the Doctor balanced calmly on the plank, crossbow not even raised to fire, was too much for Leela. Perhaps he was paralysed by fear ... For the moment everyone's eyes were fixed on the Doctor. Leela kicked the feet from under the nearest guard and made a determined dash for the control lever, tugging at it with bound hands. An angry guard shoved her away, and she fell headlong. He tried to pin her down but Leela rolled over, shot out her legs and sent him flying. She jumped to her feet—to find herself surrounded by more guards, their crossbows aimed at her heart. Leela lowered her hands and stood very still. Meanwhile the Doctor, apparently undisturbed by all this, was still balancing calmly on the plank, which by now was sagging more than ever ...

Just as it seemed about to snap, the Doctor raised his crossbow and fired. The bolt sped through the screen window, severing the rope. The shutters stopped opening, and the Doctor walked carefully along the plank towards the edge of the pit. He had almost reached safety when there came an ominous, splintering sound. As the plank broke in two, the Doctor made a desperate flying leap, just managing to land safely on the edge of the pit.

He tossed the crossbow to a guard and gave a little nod of self-congratulation. 'Very good, Doctor, very good!' He smiled at Leela. 'It was nice of you to try and help me but there was really no need.'

'Where did you learn to shoot like that?'

'Like what?' The Doctor glanced at the screen window, where the severed rope still dangled. 'Oh, like *that*! I was taught by a rather charming Swiss chap. His name was William Tell!'

The Doctor tapped a guard on the shoulder. 'Would you untie my friends please?'

The guard looked at Calib for confirmation, and Calib snapped, 'Untie them.'

The guard severed Leela's and Tomas's bonds, and the Doctor smiled round at the watching group. Calib and Andor stared silently at him, and the guards were looking at him almost in awe. It was obvious that very few survived the Test of the Horda. The Doctor guessed that his success had given him some kind of status, at least for a time. Better make use of it while

64

it lasted. 'Shall we go?' he suggested cheerfully. Before anyone could stop him, he marched confidently off to the Council hut.

Confused and frightened, Neeva was on his knees before the altar. In his ears rang the angry voice of Xoanon. 'Neeva! Neeva, where is he?'

As the Doctor entered the unseen entity seemed to become aware of him. 'Doctor? Doctor, are you there?' The voice was that of a young man.

'Yes, Xoanon, I'm here.'

At the sound of the Doctor's voice, the voice of Xoanon changed. It became deeper, more mature, and the Doctor realised he was hearing his own voice. 'Doctor, we have decided ...' Suddenly the voice changed, became youthful again—'To destroy you!'

8

Beyond the Wall

The Doctor stared thoughtfully at the space-suit, hanging scarecrow-like on its stand. He was dealing with some kind of multiple personality, he decided. Or to put it more simply, his unseen opponent was raving mad.

The Doctor decided to humour him. 'I see. Tell you what, Xoanon, why don't we meet and talk things over?'

His own voice replied. 'We are together. We have said all there is to say, and know all there is to know.'

'Perhaps so. But we don't want to do anything hasty, do we?'

'Hasty?' Then the youthful voice again. 'It's been an eternity! I'm turning off the Boundary, to let in my pets from the Beyond. Goodbye, Doctor!'

A click and then silence.

'What does it all mean?' whispered Neeva.

'Trouble,' said the Doctor. 'Large, deadly and invisible.' He lifted the disruptor gun from the altar and studied it thoughtfully.

Deep in the forest, on the Boundary, the light on top of the hidden sonic disruptor the Doctor had discovered began to flash more and more slowly. Finally it stopped altogether. All through the forest the same thing was happening to the other disruptors in their hiding places. The Boundary was no more. The village of the Sevateem lay open to attack by the invisible monsters from Beyond.

In deference to Neeva's feelings, the Doctor had carried a pile of equipment, selected from Neeva's holy relics, out of the Sanctum and into the main Council hut. He had found a set of tools, and was using it to check over the long-disused disruptor gun. Leela crouched beside him, a willing if baffled assistant. 'Screwdriver,' said the Doctor, pointing. Leela took the little tool from the kit and passed it to him.

As the Doctor made a final adjustment, Tomas came rushing in. 'We've set guards all round the perimeter, Doctor. The village has been warned. Everyone knows what to expect.'

The Doctor went on working. 'You've explained about their attraction to vibration?'

'Of course.'

The Doctor studied the jumble of technological equipment. 'We're lucky the space travellers brought so much equipment with them. Let's hope we can profit from their misfortune.'

'Space travellers?' said Leela, puzzled. 'I don't understand.'

The Doctor pointed to some letters stencilled on the tool box. 'PLANETARY SURVEY TEAM. That's where your tribe got its name. Survey Team—Sevateem.' The Doctor rubbed his chin. 'Question is— were you lot here before they arrived?'

Calib entered in time to hear the Doctor's last remark. 'I see what you mean, Doctor. Are we their captors—or their descendants?'

'You catch on quickly, Calib. Whoever they were, the travellers certainly didn't get back to base.' The Doctor paused for a moment, as if haunted by some fugitive memory. Then, shaking his head, he returned to his work.

Calib said impatiently. 'When will the weapon be ready?'

The Doctor looked up, noticing the tone of command. 'Are you taking charge, Calib?'

'Do you object?'

Leela's hand flashed to her knife. '*I* object.'

'Leela,' said Calib patiently, 'I don't. expect you to *like* me ...'

'Then you won't be disappointed. You tried to kill me—remember?'

'That is a thing to be settled between us. But now is not the time.'

The Doctor straightened up. He handed the disruptor gun, not to Calib but to Tomas. 'Here, you take this.'

Tomas took it reluctantly. It was hard to accept that this holy relic was in reality a deadly weapon. 'How does it work?'

The Doctor indicated the firing button. 'Just point and push! It's destructive up to about ten times bow range. Use it in short bursts, the power-charge will last longer.'

'Thank you, Doctor.' Holding the weapon carefully in front of him, Tomas left the hut.

68

The Doctor turned his attention to yet another piece of equipment.

'What is it, Doctor?' asked Leela.

'A stasis-beam generator. As soon as I've checked it over, we'll go and set it up.'

'Where?'

'On the Boundary, of course. Every little helps ...'

Leela kept a wary eye on the forest, while beside her the Doctor made final adjustments to the generator. All her senses were alert. The forest was silent. Perhaps the invisible monsters hadn't yet realised that the Barrier had been switched off. While she waited, Leela was sharpening her knife on a sliver of stone.

The Doctor stood up. A light was flashing on the top of the stasis-beam generator. 'There! That'll keep Xoanon's little pets away from this part of the perimeter at least. Now, we've got to find a way to get inside that Time Barrier—and soon.'

'It is hopeless, Doctor. The Old Ones tell us that the Tribe has been trying to get through the Barrier for generations.'

'I could build a time bridge of course,' said the Doctor musingly. 'But I'd have to dismantle the TARDIS, and even then it might not work ...'

'Doctor, didn't you say that nothing could go through the Barrier?'

'That's right.'

'Not even light, or sound?'

'No.'

'But Xoanon is inside the Barrier?'

69

'Yes.'

'Then how do we hear his voice?'

The Doctor jumped to his feet. 'You're a genius, Leela. A genius!'

'I am? What did I say?'

'Never mind that. Come on.'

The Doctor hurried back towards the village, and Leela followed. They dashed through the forest, through the village, across the Council hut and into Neeva's Sanctum.

Neeva sat on his sleeping platform staring vacantly into space. 'Neeva,' called the Doctor.

There was no reply. The Doctor shook him. 'Come on man, snap out of it.'

Slowly Neeva's head turned and he stared vaguely at the Doctor. 'Yes, Master, what is your will?'

'Neeva, when you hear the voice of Xoanon, is it always when you're at the altar, with the vestment hung on its frame?'

'Yes, Master.'

'Have you heard it anywhere else?'

'Yes, Master.'

'Where?'

'Yes, Master.'

The Doctor realised that Neeva was responding parrot-like, almost without thought. On a sudden inspiration, the Doctor moved away from Neeva, closer to the space-suit. Cupping his hands over his mouth he intoned, 'Neeva, Neeva! This is Xoanon.'

Neeva seemed to respond. 'Yes, Master, what is your will?'

'In what places have you heard my voice?'

70

'Only here, Master. Here in your Sanctum.'

The Doctor nodded, satisfied. 'You have been a good and faithful servant, Neeva. Go back to sleep—now!'

Neeva stretched out on his sleeping-platform and fell instantly into deep sleep.

Leela stared wonderingly. 'What's happened to him?'

'Too much, too quickly,' said the Doctor. 'He's in a state of shock.' The Doctor stood for a moment, staring into space. 'It's a tight-beam transmission, Leela, it must be.'

'What does that mean?'

'It means there is a bridge through the Barrier— and I know where it is ...'

The guard was very frightened. He had been summoned by Tomas, told that the Boundary had vanished, and ordered to patrol this stretch of the perimeter. He had lived all his life under the shelter of the Boundary, and the thought that it was no more petrified him. Ever since he was a child, he had been told of the horrors of the Beyond.

There was a rustling noise in the trees ahead. Leaves and branches started moving as something huge, invisible pushed them aside. There was deep, hoarse breathing. With a yell of sheer terror, he turned and fled.

When the man on duty at the warning gong saw the guard running towards him from the forest, being smashed and trampled into the ground by some vast, invisible force, he reacted instinctively. Grabbing his metal rod, he hammered frantically on the gong.

The Doctor and Leela were heading away from the village when they heard the clamour of the gong.

'The fools,' said Leela fiercely. 'We warned them.'

'I imagine somebody panicked.'

'They'll just attract the creatures to the village!'

'We can't help them now, Leela. It's up to Tomas and the disruptor gun. Come on, time's running out.'

They ran on through the forest.

The guard was still beating frantically on the gong when Andor ran up and wrested the metal rod away from him. 'Stop that, you idiot. You'll attract more of them.'

The guard pointed. 'Something killed one of the guards. I saw it, it's coming towards us from the edge of the forest.'

Andor was growing old, but he was still a chief. 'Come on, Tomas, we must warn the other guards,' he said, and set off towards the forest.

All was silent as they reached the forest edge and moved past the crushed body of the guard. Andor started to move forward into the trees.

'Andor, be careful,' called Tomas. 'It must be still about.' Suddenly the bushes close to Andor began thrashing furiously and there was a savage roar.

'Look out,' yelled Tomas, but he was too late. Some

72

vast invisible force gripped Andor, sweeping him off his feet as though snatched up by invisible claws.

Tomas ran in as close as he dared, raised the disruptor gun and fired.

There was a crackle of power and a scream of rage and pain from the invisible monster, as it flung Andor to the ground. As it retreated the creature was momentarily visible, outlined in a vivid yellow glare of light.

Tomas caught a glimpse of a giant face. It was hideously distorted—but unmistakably the face of the Doctor.

Tomas ran to Andor, who lay crumpled on the ground, his body shattered by the impact of his fall.

Tomas knelt beside him. 'Andor! Andor!' he called.

For a moment Andor raised his head. 'Xoanon, save me,' he muttered weakly, and fell back, dead.

There came a shattering roar of anger, and the trees began tossing once more. Tomas looked up, realising that the monster must be rushing back towards him.

He raised the disruptor gun, fired a rapid burst, then turned and fled back towards the village.

The Doctor and Leela had crossed the valley by now. They stood at the foot of the mountain, staring up at the great carved head.

'The nose should be a shade more aquiline,' said the Doctor judiciously. 'And the classic proportion of the brow hasn't been perfectly executed. Still we mustn't complain, we live in an imperfect universe.'

Leela said practically. 'Where's the bridge through

the Barrier, then? Up the nose?'

'Certainly not. It's over the teeth and down the throat.' They started to climb.

A long, weary time later they stood directly beneath the enormous chin. The Doctor perched on a boulder, leaped and clung, hauling himself over the rampart of the giant teeth. Leela followed him, and he pulled her to safety. They stood up and looked around. They were in a kind of irregular tunnel, leading downwards. It stretched for a considerable distance, with a gleam of light at the end.

'Odd feeling, this,' said the Doctor.

'What is?'

'Standing in your own throat!'

Leela and the Doctor moved cautiously forward. They were some way down the tunnel when there was a junction, and from it a light was moving towards them.

'What is it?' whispered Leela.

The Doctor put a finger to his lips for silence.

They waited silently as the light came nearer. A hulking distorted shadow appeared on the wall ...

9

The Tesh

'Tomas! Tomas, over here.'

Tomas checked his panic-stricken rush through the forest and listened. Calib appeared from behind a tree-trunk, and Tomas went over to join him.

'I heard the noise,' whispered Calib. 'What was it?'

'The Evil One,' gasped Tomas. 'It was huge ... It killed Andor.'

Characteristically, Calib's first thoughts were of his own advantage. 'Then I'm leader now.'

'And where will you lead us, Calib?' Before Calib could reply Tomas said, 'Listen!' There was a trampling sound deep in the forest behind them. They could see tree-tops waving and hear deep, hoarse breathing. 'That thing's on the move again.'

Calib looked at the heavy disruptor gun in Tomas's hands. 'But the weapon worked?'

'It revealed the Evil One's face, and drove it away—for a time.'

Calib's mind was busy with his new responsibilities. 'We must get back to the village. If we move quietly it may pass us by.'

The Doctor and Leela watched the distorted shadow come closer.

'What is it?' whispered Leela again.

'There's only one way to find out.' Keeping flat against the wall they edged along until they could see down the side-tunnel. An extraordinary figure was moving slowly towards them. It wore some kind of all-over protective suit with helmet and gauntlets. Instinctively Leela raised her crossbow, but the Doctor put a restraining hand on her arm.

The figure stopped and turned. For a moment it stood facing a stretch of blank tunnel wall. It took a sudden pace forward, and suddenly it was bathed in green light. Then it vanished.

Leela gave a gasp of astonishment. 'It's gone? Where did it go?'

She ran forward to look at the patch of wall. The Doctor went on past her, down to the other end of the tunnel, where light was pouring through the far entrance. For a long time the Doctor stood staring at the view of the world beyond the Barrier.

He was looking out on to arid rocky plain, illuminated by the harsh glare of the planet's two suns. In its centre stood a huge rocket ship, its harsh, functional lines sweeping skywards like a great tower of steel. 'Now I remember,' breathed the Doctor. 'The Mordee expedition. And I thought I was helping them!' He stood as if in a trance as the memories flooded back into his mind.

Leela's voice broke into his reverie. 'Doctor, what are you doing? Why don't you come and help me find the Tesh?'

Slowly the Doctor walked back along the tunnel. 'Tesh? How do you know it was a Tesh? Have you ever seen a Tesh?'

Leela was bemused by the barrage of questions. 'Its skin was loose and shiny, as we were told. And it had two heads, one inside the other.'

'That was a protective suit. Must be a different environment in there.' The Doctor took a step forward, a green light bathed his body and he disappeared.

Leela jumped back terrified, making the sign of protection. The Doctor's impatient voice came through the wall. 'Come on, then!'

'How can I? It's a solid wall.'

'Nonsense, it's an illusion. It's called a psi-tri projection, a three-dimensional image which deceives the eye. Close both eyes, take one step back, then just walk forward.'

Leela shut her eyes tightly, and obeyed. She moved forward expecting every minute to crash into the wall. Instead, she bumped into the Doctor. She opened her eyes to find herself in a small metal-walled chamber, the Doctor beside her. Leela stared round incredulously. 'Great Xoanon, where are we?'

'It's called an anti-grav transporter. It'll take us to the ship in no time at all.'

The capsule vibrated slightly, and began to move ...

Inside the swirling chaos of light that was the fragmented mind of Xoanon, voices were speaking. Male and female, young and old, together and separate, they blended into an ecstatic chorus. 'We are here. We are returned. Now we shall be one. We are here. We are returned. Now we shall be one. Now we must destroy us. Now we must destroy us and become one.'

The voices rose to a frenzied chant. 'Now we must destroy us and become *one* ... *one* ... *one*!'

The capsule stopped, a door slid open, and the Doctor and Leela emerged. They found themselves in a short metal corridor. It ended in another door, which also slid open before them. The Doctor stepped confidently through, and Leela followed, crossbow at the ready.

They were in the main control room of the space ship, but a control room which had been fantastically transformed. Instrument consoles were draped with elaborately decorated tapestries, monitor screens garlanded with flowers, like the idols in some jungle temple. Joss sticks and ceremonial candles burned before rows of controls.

'It's a shrine,' whispered Leela,

'I'm afraid so ... It seems the Tesh are as ignorant of their origins as your own people.'

'And what are their origins?'

'How does the Litany go? The bit about Paradise, I mean.'

Leela stared at him, and the Doctor said impatiently, 'You said you learned it as a child. You said you *knew* it ...'

'I do, I do ...' Leela began to recite. 'The Seva-teem were sent forth by god to seek Paradise. The Tesh remained at the Place of Land ...'

'Well, there you are. In other words, the Sevateem explored the planet, the Tesh stayed to work on the ship in the place where it landed. Here.'

Leela struggled to take it all in. 'Then we're the same people?'

'That's right. The Tesh were the technicians and the Sevateem were the survey team. You're all human beings from this colonist ship.'

'Then what happened to us, Doctor? *What happened?*'

'I'm afraid I did.'

The Doctor stood staring into space, remembering. It had been somewhere near the beginning of that business with the Giant Robot. The Doctor had just undergone his latest regeneration. The early days of a new incarnation are always a tricky period for a Time Lord, and in this case the process had been hurriedly accelerated in order to save his life. He had been in a confused, irresponsible state, his new personality still not fully established. Even now his memories of those first days were hazy. There had been Sarah, and the Brigadier, and the problem of the Robot to grapple with ... And all the time there had been this overwhelming urge to go off into the TARDIS and just disappear. One night the urge had been too strong and the Doctor had given way. He had sped off alone in the TARDIS to another time and another planet—this planet. He had found the colonists in trouble, repaired their computer with careless expertise and gone on his way—leaving, he now realised, a terrible legacy behind him. Since the TARDIS had returned him to Earth within minutes of his departure, no one ever knew that he'd been away.

Indeed, he himself had almost forgotten the strange dream-like interlude. But somehow his unconscious mind knew—and it had brought him back to this planet to undo the harm he had done.

Vaguely the Doctor became aware of Leela's voice. 'Answer me, Doctor. What did you do?'

'I misunderstood what Xoanon was.'

'Is he a human being?'

'At the time I didn't realise he was a being at all.' The Doctor flicked dials on a nearby console. 'These instruments are dead ...'

'What did you think Xoanon was?' persisted Leela.

Before the Doctor could answer, a strange figure appeared from the rear of the control room. He was tall and thin, white-haired with a thin, lined face. The simple robes he wore gave him the air of some kind of priest. He bowed and smiled. 'Welcome, Lord.' His voice was soft and gentle.

The Doctor looked curiously at him. For all his mild manner there was a feeling of tremendous power about this man. Power rigidly controlled, held in check. Despite the quiet voice and the friendly smile, he had the fierce, burning eyes of a fanatic.

The man took another step forward. Instinctively Leela raised her bow to cover him.

At once the man's face changed, becoming hard and set. He stared coldly at Leela. Suddenly she found her muscles locked in the grip of some invisible force. Fighting every inch of the way she sank slowly to her knees.

The Doctor grabbed the man by the shoulder, and shook him. 'Will you please stop doing that?'

The man pulled away from the Doctor and Leela slumped to the ground.

The Doctor ran to her and knelt by her side. She was quite unconscious. He heard the calm voice of the stranger. 'She is not damaged. My acolytes will attend to her.'

Two more men, both wearing similar robes, both with the same fanatical look about them, came into the control room, picked up Leela and started to carry her away. The Doctor moved to block their path. 'Where are they taking her?'

'She will be tended. We recognise her value, Lord.'

His tone was calm, and utterly sincere. Reassured the Doctor let the men take Leela off. He turned and the newcomer knelt at his feet, head bowed.

With some embarrassment the Doctor said, 'Er, have you dropped something?'

'I do you honour, Lord of Time. We have waited long for your return.'

'I see,' said the Doctor thoughtfully. 'Well, thank you for the honour, but it's really information I need at present. Do get up.'

The man raised his head, but did not rise.

The Doctor looked down at him. 'What's your name?'

'I am Jabel, Lord, Captain of the People of Tesh.'

The Doctor realised that his questions would have to be framed in a way that Jabel could accept and understand. 'Tell me, Jabel, do *your* people have a holy purpose?'

'Yes, Lord,' said Jabel proudly. 'We serve Xoanon and tend the holy places. We guard this Tower against the Savage. We deny the flesh that our minds may find communion with Xoanon.'

The Doctor began striding about the control room. 'Yes, there's a sort of logic. Outside the Barrier physical courage and strength. Inside, paraphysical development, the sort of mental power you used on Leela. Selective breeding—it's an experiment in eugenics!'

'Yes, Lord,' agreed Jabel meekly.

The Doctor stopped his pacing, realising that Jabel was still on his knees. 'Oh do get up, that floor must be very hard. Did no one ever tell you kneeling stunts your growth?'

Slowly Jabel rose. His eyes were troubled, as if somehow the Doctor wasn't quite what he'd expected.

'Now then, Jabel,' said the Doctor briskly. 'Do you know where Xoanon is?'

'Yes, Lord.'

'Where?'

'He is in no one place, Lord. He is all around us, everywhere.'

The Doctor sighed. 'So you don't know. I didn't think you did.'

'You and he are as one, Lord. You will show us the Way.'

The Doctor was in no mood for mysticism. 'Do you know what a computer is?'

'No, Lord,' said Jabel, still with the same infuriating calm.

The Doctor began ripping the ornamental draperies from the control panels. 'I've got to find that thing before it kills us all.'

When Leela recovered she was lying on a metal table in a metal-walled room. Above her was suspended an elaborate array of sinister-looking apparatus. She struggled to get up, and found herself fixed to the table by metal clamps. A low electronic hum came from the instruments above her, as if machinery was warming up. There was a low chime, and a calm female voice said, 'Final warning, final warning. Particle analyser has entered terminal phase countdown. All personnel please clear the area.'

Leela struggled wildly, but the metal clamps held her fast.

The Doctor rampaged round the control room, testing keyboards and switches in vain. 'This whole control room has been disconnected. On a ship this size it could take me days to find the central complex.' He looked at Jabel again. If he could frame the question in a way that Jabel could understand ...

'I must be slipping,' he muttered to himself. 'Jabel, where is the holy of holies?'

'All of the Place of Land is holy.'

'There must be somewhere on this ship where no one's allowed to go. A kind of Inner Sanctum.'

'Yes, Lord,' said Jabel promptly. 'The Sacred Chamber.'

The Doctor gave a sigh of relief. 'Yes, that's what I mean. Where is it?'

'On level thirty-seven, Lord.'

The Doctor's fiddling with controls had not been entirely without result. A monitor screen had come to life. On it he could see Leela, strapped to a metal table. 'What's going on? What are they doing to her?'

'Particle analysis, Lord. We shall reduce the subject to its constituent parts.'

'But that will kill her!'

'Yes, Lord. But she is only a Savage.'

'That's not a good enough reason!' Frantically the Doctor began hunting for an off button for the analyser.

Jabel stared at the Doctor in puzzlement, unable to understand his concern. 'At intervals the Savages have power to open the Barrier. The particle analyser may tell us how they do it. Surely that is why you brought her to us?'

'The Savages don't open the Barrier, you lack-brain,' said the Doctor furiously. 'Xoanon does. Do you understand? Xoanon!'

For the first time Jabel showed emotion. 'You lie!'

'Give the order to stop that particle analyser,' commanded the Doctor.

'You are not the Lord of Time, come again to save us!'

'Will you give that order?'

'No! You are a blasphemer, an impostor.'

The Doctor began groping in his pockets. 'Right then, I'll go and deal with it myself.'

He was turning to leave the control room when Jabel fixed him with a sudden fierce stare. The Doctor went down, as if struck by a heavy club.

10

The Summons

An urgent voice was shouting in the Doctor's ear. 'Doctor, Doctor, please wake up!' He opened his eyes to find himself strapped to a metal table next to Leela.

A danger light was flashing on the wall beside them, and a countdown clock showed there were only seconds to go before the machine would dissolve them to constituent particles, killing them in the process. Leela saw the Doctor twist round frantically, aiming something in his hand at the battery of lights and projectors above them. The last second of countdown ticked away, and a fierce ray of light beamed down on them from above. There was a sudden explosion, a shower of sparks, the machinery above them went dead, and the clamps holding them to the table sprang open.

A little gingerly the Doctor sat up. 'Be thankful you're living and trust to your luck, and march to your front like a soldier,' he said solemnly. 'Kipling— or was it Gertrude Stein? Someone like that, anyway.' He helped Leela down from the table.

She looked up unbelievingly at the charred and twisted machinery above them. 'I think you've broken it. How did you manage that?'

The Doctor held out his hand and showed her a

small metal mirror in the palm. 'To be strictly accurate, it broke itself. Luckily this was already in my hand when Jabel knocked me out. All I did was reflect the power back with it. Still, I don't suppose the owners will see it that way. We'd better be off!'

Jabel stood waiting in the control room. Gentek, his chief acolyte, entered and bowed low. 'They have escaped, Captain,' he said calmly. All display of emotion was forbidden amongst the People of Tesh.

With equal calm Jabel said, 'They must be found and killed. This will take precedence over all other duties and devotions.'

Gentek bowed again. 'Then he is not the Lord of Time, the One Who Will Return?'

'He is our enemy and the enemy of Xoanon. Kill him—and the Savage.'

Gentek bowed again, Jabel returned the bow, and the acolyte left the control room.

Jabel moved slowly over to the nearest console. His face remained calm and composed then suddenly he smashed his fist down on to the console.

The sudden flare of emotion over, he resumed his measured pacing of the control room.

The Doctor and Leela ducked back out of sight as an acolyte armed with a blaster hurried past the end of the corridor.

'He seems to be looking for something,' said the Doctor.

'Us?'

'Very probably.'

'Doctor, you didn't finish telling me. What is Xoanon?'

'A machine that became a living creature. An omniscient computer with acute schizophrenia—not a very pretty thought, is it? And all my fault.'

'*How* is it your fault?'

'When I was here before, the Mordee were having trouble with their new computer. I repaired and reprogrammed it for them. Unfortunately I forgot to wipe my personality prints from the data core ... or did I really forget? I forget if I forgot or not ...'

'You're not making yourself very clear, Doctor.'

'Well, I wasn't quite myself at the time. It may just have been my own egotism. Anyway, now the computer has a split personality, and part of it is mine. Now, is that clear?'

'No,' said Leela.

'Oh well, never mind. Let's get moving again.' As they moved away, a sensor in the wall glowed brightly.

In the glowing sphere at the centre of Xoanon's brain was a picture of the Doctor and Leela moving away down the corridor. 'Us within us,' crooned Xoanon softly. 'Soon we shall make two, one.' There was a peal of mad laughter.

It was very dark in the forest, and the air was full of the screams of dying men, and the bellowing of invisible monsters. Moving quietly through the darkness, Tomas lifted the disruptor gun and fired at the nearest sound. There was a scream of pain and the invisible creature retreated. Tomas fired again, and the gun went dead. He had used the weapon once too often. Its power-charge was exhausted. Tossing the gun aside, Tomas ran to find Calib, who was hiding nearby. 'The gun is useless now, Calib. The power's used up.'

'Well, at least we've drawn them away from the village. Now we must fall back. Get the men moving, Tomas—and quietly.'

The Doctor led Leela down yet another corridor, pausing by the open door of a small room packed with electronic equipment. Lines of monitor screens covered one wall, storage cupboards and lockers the others. He beckoned to Leela. 'Come in and shut the door.'

Leela obeyed. 'Where are we?'

'Auxiliary Communications Room and Stores,' said the Doctor briskly. 'I imagine Xoanon keeps an eye on everything. Let's see what's going on outside.'

The Doctor's hands flickered over the controls and suddenly one of the screens lit up. It showed Calib, Tomas and a handful of warriors making their way back towards the village. Close behind them the trees were shaken by the movement of the huge invisible monsters.

'Look, it's near the edge of the village,' whispered Leela. 'And the phantoms are still chasing them.

They must have got through from the Beyond.'

'Looks like it,' said the Doctor sadly. 'I didn't expect that stasis-beam to hold them forever. They're projections from the dark side of Xoanon's id. Tremendously powerful, with enough kinetic energy to kill!'

Leela made for the door. 'I'm going back!'

'Don't be absurd. What do you think you can do?'

'We've got to do something to help!'

The Doctor said. 'Xoanon won't let his creatures cross the Time Barrier. Your friends will be safer inside, if I can arrange it.' He began studying the controls.

'What about the Tesh?'

'I didn't say they'd be safe—just safer.' The Doctor flicked another switch. 'Neeva! Neeva! Wake up, Neeva!'

To Leela's astonishment Neeva's voice came through a nearby speaker. 'Yes, Master?'

'Neeva,' said the Doctor impressively, 'this is Xoanon.'

'What is your will, Master?'

'Tell Calib to lead the people through the mouth of the—the head carved on the mountain.'

'Through the mouth of the idol, Master? Will Calib believe that this is truly your command?'

The Doctor thought for a moment. 'You will say these words to him: "I don't believe in ghosts either." '

' "I don't believe in ghosts either," ' repeated Neeva.

'That's right. Go now and do my will.'

'Yes ... Doctor,' said Neeva's voice. Then there was silence.

The Doctor grinned. 'I underestimated that man! And now, Leela, we've got an appointment on level thirty-seven.'

Gentek came into the control room and bowed before Jabel. 'They cannot be found.'

'Continue the search.'

Gentek bowed again and turned to leave, but Jabel called him back. 'Gentek! Is the guard posted outside the Sacred Chamber?'

'Yes, Captain.'

Gentek left the control room. Jabel stood waiting calmly, trusting in the will of Xoanon.

The Doctor and Leela emerged from a lift and hurried along yet another featureless metal corridor. 'This is level thirty-seven,' said the Doctor. 'If I've counted right, that is!'

The corridor led to another wider one. They peeped round the corner and saw a set of massive steel doors, guarded by a Tesh with a disruptor gun. He looked alert and wary. There was no chance of getting past him unseen.

They dodged back out of sight. The Doctor considered for a moment, took off his hat and handed it to Leela. She looked puzzled, then gave a delighted smile. Luring an enemy into an ambush was just the sort of thing she liked.

Conscious of his great responsibility, the Tesh guarding the Sacred Chamber looked keenly up and down the corridor. He heard a whispered 'Psst!' and swung round, gun at the ready. A strange black object appeared round the corner for a second, at about the height of a tall man. It remained visible for a few seconds then drew back out of sight. 'Aliens!' thought the guard excitedly. He would win great praise from Jabel if he destroyed them.

Cautiously he crept towards the corridor junction, eyes fixed on the spot where the black shape had appeared. When he was near enough he sprang round the corner, gun raised to fire—and saw only blank wall. He saw a flicker of movement below his eye level, and realised too late that his enemy was crouched down low. He caught a brief glimpse of a skin-clad Savage and lowered the gun to fire.

Ducking under the gun, Leela caught the astonished Tesh by the sleeves of his robe, bent, twisted and threw. The Tesh hurtled over her shoulder, his head thudding into the corridor wall.

The Doctor picked up his hat, dusted it carefully and put it back on his head. He picked up the gun and handed it to Leela. 'Keep watch?'

'Can't I come with you?'

The Doctor shook his head. 'Xoanon's—well, unstable, to put it mildly. He might kill me—and he'd certainly kill you. Anyway, we need someone on guard.

The Doctor went up to the great doors and touched a control. The doors slid silently open. He passed through, and they closed behind him.

11

Xoanon

Calib and Tomas were climbing up to the mouth of the giant head on the mountain.

Neeva's message had been received with doubt and suspicion. Most of the Sevateem thought it was a trap devised by the Evil One.

By now the invisible monsters were rampaging through the village smashing the flimsy huts to fragments. Most of the Tribe had fled into the forest and were crouching motionless and silent in whatever hiding-places they could find.

Besides Neeva himself, only Calib and Tomas had been willing to obey the message. Tomas because he had hopes of finding Leela again, Calib because he was staking everything on this final gamble. If he could lead the Sevateem to victory his hold on the Chieftainship would be assured.

Only a handful of warriors could be persuaded to accompany them. They were waiting now with Neeva, beneath the head of the idol, while Calib and Tomas scouted ahead. Calib had little taste for putting himself in danger—but he knew that a show of heroism was needed to impress his people.

Calib clambered over the great stone teeth, and turned and pulled Tomas up beside him. He drew a deep breath. 'Well, the tunnel's here, let's take a look.' They moved cautiously down the long tunnel, Calib in the lead. Suddenly the figure of a Tesh appeared from the darkness ahead. He wore the sinister-looking protective suit, and the disruptor gun in his hands was raised to fire. Calib stood frozen in terror.

'Calib, look out!' yelled Tomas. Calib jumped aside, Tomas's arm flashed down, and a heavy knife thudded into the heart of the Tesh. He gasped and slid silently down the wall. Calib darted forward and snatched the gun. He turned to Tomas, who was recovering his knife. 'Keep your eyes open. Where there's one Tesh there's likely to be more.'

From the forest below them there floated the distant sound of shattering trees, and the roar of the invisible monsters.

'The creatures are catching up with us,' said Tomas worriedly. 'We've got to get the men inside the Barrier quickly.'

'All right. Go back and get them moving, Tomas. I'll wait here.' Clutching the disruptor gun, Calib stared nervously into the darkness ahead.

For a moment the Doctor stood in total darkness. A pattern of swirling multicoloured lights appeared in the darkness ahead of him, and he began walking slowly towards them. As he moved forward he began to hear voices, thousands of them it seemed, chattering, whispering, screaming. Gradually the voices seemed to blend, to merge into one compelling voice that filled the darkness all around him, coming from nowhere and from everywhere. 'Who are you? Who are you? Who are you?' demanded the voice.

The Doctor shouted. 'I'm the Doctor!'

There was instant silence. The lights disappeared, and the Doctor was plunged into darkness again. Then a harsh white beam shone from the darkness, seeming to fix him to the spot where he stood.

'Who are you?' said another voice. It was a woman's voice, soft and gentle.

'Who are you?' said the voice of a young man.

'Who are you?' said a third voice—and the Doctor knew it was Xoanon's voice. Yet it was his own voice too. 'I am the Doctor,' he repeated.

'Why have you come, Doctor?'

'To correct a mistake I made when I was here long ago.'

'We have made no mistake.' The voice split and fragmented again, tuning into a kind of chorus. 'No mistake ... no mistake ... no mistake ...' chanted the voices eerily.

'*I* made the mistake,' said the Doctor. 'When the ship first landed here, the new experimental computer failed. I thought the data core must have been damaged in the landing. So I renewed it by using a direct link with the compatible centres in my own brain.'

'The Sidelian memory transfer,' said Xoanon's voice.

'A variation of it, yes.'

'Good, very good,' said Xoanon approvingly.

The Doctor was about to go on when the personality

of Xoanon split once more. 'How did he find the ship?' demanded the youthful voice.

'Sssh,' reproved the female voice. 'Don't interrupt, you'll spoil the story!'

The Doctor groaned inwardly. When Xoanon's concentration wandered, his personality split into its divergent parts. It was like holding a conversation with an unruly crowd—a crowd of madmen.

'This isn't a fairy tale,' shouted the Doctor. 'It actually happened. And it's vitally important to you, Xoanon. You've got to listen to me.'

Leela knew that it wouldn't take long for the Tesh to find her, and when the first head appeared, round the corner, she was ready. She fired a rapid burst, and the head disappeared.

Leela considered her position. She was in a kind of blind alley, the doors to the Sacred Chamber at her back. There were only two places an attack could come from, the far end of the main corridor, and the junction point with the smaller corridor to her right, where she had just shot down the Tesh.

Another Tesh appeared at the far end, and Leela fired instantly. He fell, another Tesh appeared round the nearby corner and she fired again. 'Three down,' she thought exultantly. Full of the joy of battle, she waited, scanning the corridor ahead.

Screwing up his eyes against the blinding light, the Doctor continued his attempt to communicate with the rational part of Xoanon's personality. 'The computer was a new, experimental model. For generations teams of technicians had worked on it trying to extend its power. Finally, without realising it, they had created life. The computer hadn't failed at all. It had evolved the first of a completely new species.'

'A new species?' said the youthful voice mockingly. 'Oh, come now, Doctor!'

Xoanon's attention was slipping again, and the Doctor increased the urgency in his voice. 'Yes, a new species. When I came, it was still in shock. I simply didn't recognise the birth trauma—that was my mistake. When I connected my brain to the new-born creature, it didn't just take compatible information as a machine would have done. It took everything!'

'Fascinating,' said Xoanon politely. 'May I ask a question?' The voice changed, answered itself. 'Sssh, let him finish,' said the youth.

Determinedly the Doctor went on. 'When the computer woke it had a complete personality. Mine. It thought I was itself—until it began to develop another separate self—its own self. That was when it started to go mad.'

'And where is it, Doctor?' said Xoanon's voice, in a tone of polite enquiry. 'Where is this poor, mad, mad machine creature?'

The Doctor drew a deep breath. Was Xoanon stable enough to accept the truth? 'It's here, Xoanon. I'm talking to it. It's you.'

There was a moment of silence. The beam of light dimmed slowly until at last the Doctor found himself once more in darkness. 'Xoanon?' he called softly. 'Xoanon?'

The youth's voice spoke. 'I grow tired,' it said sulkily. 'I will think you no longer, Doctor.'

'No, wait, Xoanon,' shouted the Doctor. 'I'm the Doctor. I am real. I am separate. You must acknowledge me.'

'I will not think you,' screamed the voice. 'We are Xoanon.'

'You are Xoanon, and I am the Doctor.' He shouted it again and again, in an attempt to force Xoanon to accept the reality of his existence. 'I am the Doctor! I am the Doctor! I am the Doctor!'

'No,' screamed Xoanon. 'No! No! No!'

A tiny spot of light appeared in the distance. It expanded and came closer, became a face. The Doctor's own face, distorted with rage and hate.

In a hundred different voices Xoanon screamed his fury, his determination to deny the Doctor's very existence. 'No,' howled the maddened voice. 'No, no, no, no, no!'

The face came nearer and nearer, grew larger and larger. Soon it was enormous, filling the entire chamber, eyes bulging, mouth twisted in a scream of terror.

The Doctor felt the storm of madness swirl round him, swallow him up. He buried his face in his hands to escape the terrifying sight, but there was no escape. There was nothing in the universe but the face and voice of Xoanon.

The Doctor collapsed, writhing in agony, the voice of Xoanon filling his brain. 'Who am I? Who am I? WHO AM I?'

12

The Trap

Leela's enemies were too many now for her to risk trying to pick them off one by one. Instead she laid down a steady barrage of fire, sweeping corridor end and corner alternately, forcing the enemy to keep their heads down all the time.

It was an effective enough method, but it had one big disadvantage—as Leela realised when her disrupter gun stuttered and died. She had exhausted the charge.

She tossed down the gun, drew her knife, and waited. After a moment a Tesh head appeared cautiously round the corner. When there was no shot from Leela, the head appeared again. More Tesh appeared, and still more. They advanced steadily towards Leela, covering her with their guns. She wondered why they didn't shoot and get it over with. Perhaps they'd been ordered to take her alive. Well, they wouldn't find it easy. It would cost a few Tesh lives before they subdued her.

The Tesh came steadily onward, Leela crouched, knife in hand, poised to spring—and the lights in the corridor flickered.

The Tesh halted, looking uneasily at each other. The lights flickered again, and then went out. In the darkness Leela heard cries of fear and the sound of panic-stricken retreat. Other lights came on, dim reddish ones, and Leela saw that the Tesh were fleeing down the corridor. She ran forward and sprang, bringing down the nearest before he could get away. To her astonishment he made no attempt to struggle. Instead he remained crouching face-down, his hands over his face.

Leela sheathed her knife, snatched the gun from his unresisting hands. 'Tesh! What is happening?' She prodded him with her foot.

The Tesh made no reply. Leela dropped to one knee and shoved the gun close to his ear. 'Answer, while you still have a head to answer with!'

The man was moaning with fear. 'It is the Light of Failsafe!'

'What does it mean?'

'The end of the world!'

'Why?' She jabbed him with the gun. 'Why Tesh?'

'It means death and destruction. It happened before, at the Time of Land.' He crouched low, moaning with fear.

Leela turned away contemptuously. 'Cowering down there won't help you.' She decided it was time to find the Doctor. Touching the control, she went through the great steel doors.

Immediately she was assailed by a barrage of lights and sound. Xoanon was still screaming his agonised question. 'Who am I? Who am I? Who am I?'

The Doctor writhed on the floor, hands over his ears, trying in vain to block out the sound of Xoanon's voice. The huge distorted vision of the Doctor's face hung in mid-air like a demon mask.

Leela brought up her gun and fired, and the demon face exploded in a swirl of colours. All at once there was darkness and silence.

Leela groped her way towards the Doctor who lay out on the floor, apparently unconscious. Grabbing him by the shoulders she started lugging him towards the door.

As she dragged him along, swirling lights appeared in the darkness and there was a low babble of voices. Xoanon was coming back to life.

As they came into the corridor the Doctor came to life as well. Leela helped him to his feet, and he was able to stagger the last few steps. The door closed behind them and he leaned thankfully against it, gasping for breath.

Leela looked at him in concern. 'Are you all right, Doctor?'

'I think so. Are you all right? What happened to you?' Leela told him of her battle with the Tesh, and its unexpected end. The Doctor said, 'Xoanon's little tantrum must have triggered off the Ship's emergency procedures.'

'Was that Xoanon—that thing that looked like you?'

'Yes, part of him. Everything behind that door is Xoanon. You were inside him. Most powerful computer ever built.'

'Why was he trying to hurt you, Doctor?'

'He's insane,' said the Doctor simply.

'What will he do now?'

'I imagine his first impulse will be to kill me. That

will be more important to him than anything else.'

'Why does he hate you so much?'

'I contradict what he thinks is real. I'm a threat to his world.' The Doctor straightened up and looked round. 'Still the emergency lighting and something else ...' He sniffed. 'A smell of ... a smell of a smell!'

Leela sniffed too. 'There *is* something. It seemed to come from the corridor wall.' She reached out her hand, but the Doctor knocked it away. 'Don't touch that!'

He fished an old Roman denarius from his pocket and tossed it against the metal wall. There was a bright blue flash and a crackle of sparks. 'Xoanon must have shorted the main power circuit through the walls.'

(Further down the corridor, the terrified Tesh was still crouching where Leela had left him. Suddenly he tensed, then rose slowly to his feet. He began walking along the corridor towards Leela and the Doctor who were studying the electrified wall.)

'As traps go, a bit haphazard,' said the Doctor. 'I'd have expected something more positive ...'

The Tesh flung himself at him, seizing him by the throat. The sudden ferocity of the attack took the Doctor completely by surprise, and he fell back choking. He recovered and tried to break free, but his attacker had super-normal strength. He also had a definite purpose. Slowly but surely he was dragging the Doctor towards the electrified wall.

'This really isn't necessary,' gasped the Doctor. 'Tell you what, I've got a wonderful idea ...'

Not daring to fire in case she hit the Doctor, Leela threw down the gun, and tried to drag the Tesh away.

He gave her a savage blow in the stomach, and she fell back gasping. The Tesh returned to the struggle with the Doctor, dragging him to the ground. They rolled over and over, coming closer and closer to the wall. Clearly the Tesh had no objection to sacrificing his own life in order to kill the Doctor.

Inches away from the wall, the Doctor managed to wriggle beneath his attacker. He gave a desperate heave.

The Tesh thudded into the wall and died in a blaze of blue sparks.

The Doctor struggled to his feet and looked sadly down at the body. 'Why wouldn't he listen ...'

'He acted like one possessed by a demon.'

'Yes ... I'm afraid Xoanon's just warming up. When he gets desperate enough he's going to destroy everything, just to get at me. There's not much time.'

The Doctor hurried off down the corridor. Picking up the disrupter gun, Leela followed. As they moved off, the red lights dimmed and the lighting returned to normal.

At the far end of the tunnel through the giant head, Calib, Tomas, Neeva, and a handful of warriors stood gazing out at the world beyond the Barrier. Like the Doctor before them they saw a barren plain and a towering space ship.

Tomas said reverently. 'At last, we're here.'

Calib smiled wryly. 'And I always believed it was only legend ...' Neeva came forward to join them, staring intently at the rocket ship. He began reciting from the Litany. 'The gates of Paradise shall be open to the people of Xoanon, and his dwelling place revealed.'

Tomas looked sharply at him. 'We've outgrown the old superstitions, Neeva.'

'But it's there, isn't it, Tomas,' said Neeva. 'We start getting proof, and we stop believing.'

'When there's proof you don't need to believe.'

Calib interrupted them. 'Get the men ready, Tomas. We're going to climb down there and capture that Tower. This is one attack that isn't going to fail. I wish Andor were here now to see us destroy the Tesh.'

'The Tesh—and Xoanon.' Neeva's eyes glittered feverishly, and there was hysteria in his voice. 'Xoanon is our real enemy. He betrayed me—and I'm going to kill him.'

The Doctor led Leela back to the auxiliary control room, closing the door behind them. He began fishing through the various lockers and cupboards, pulling out an astonishing variety of electronic spare parts. He selected certain specific items, and began stowing them away in his roomy pockets. 'You know, Leela,' he said, 'the very powerful and the very stupid have one thing in common ...'

Leela wasn't listening. She stiffened suddenly, her eyes widened, and slowly she swung her disruptor gun round to cover the Doctor.

'You see,' the Doctor went on, 'they don't alter their view to fit the facts. They alter the facts to fit their views ... which can be very uncomfortable if you happen to be one of the facts that need altering.'

Leela's finger tightened on her trigger.

Hurt by her lack of response to his rather neat turn of phrase, the Doctor looked up, and caught sight of Leela's reflection in one of the unused viewing screens. He ducked and the disruptor beam sizzled over his head, shattering the screen.

Still moving with the same zombie-like deliberation, Leela swung round towards him. The Doctor jumped across the control room and took shelter behind a control console. Leela began stalking slowly towards him—and the Doctor started fishing hastily through his pockets. Hurriedly he produced his sonic screwdriver, and a large, oddly-shaped crystal.

Just as Leela appeared over the top of the console, gun raised, the Doctor touched the crystal with the sonic screwdriver, and it gave out a clear, ringing note.

Leela froze. Cautiously the Doctor went to her. She was standing quite still, staring straight ahead. 'The gun is getting heavy,' said the Doctor softly. 'It is heavy ... heavy ... heavy ...'

Slowly Leela lowered the gun. 'When I count to three, you will wake. One ... two ... three.' On three the Doctor tapped the crystal again, and the ringing stopped.

Leela blinked at the Doctor, and he gave her a reassuring smile, as he returned screwdriver and crystal to his pocket. 'I think I've got everything I need. Shall we go?'

Leela gave him a puzzled stare, and rubbed a hand over her eyes.

'Something wrong?' asked the Doctor.

'I was by the door. Now I'm over here. I don't remember moving.'

'You're probably tired. Do you remember how to get to the main control room?'

'Yes, I think so.'

'Then lead the way!'

As Jabel knelt in meditation before the holy relics of Xoanon, Gentek burst in, babbling with panic. 'Savages are attacking the main airlock,' he screamed. 'They will soon gain entry to the Tower! What must we do?'

Jabel rose and looked at Gentek with cold distaste. 'And is that your excuse for behaving like a degenerate savage yourself?'

Gentek drew a deep, shuddering breath as he struggled for control. 'Forgive me, Captain, but——'

'You are an acolyte of the People of Tesh, one of the chosen of Xoanon. Will he accept into communion an unreasoning brute, a mindless beast?'

Gentek gave a low ritual bow. 'I accept my fault and seek forgiveness. My mind and flesh which should be Two were One, and the Way was hid by Blood.'

Jabel returned the bow. 'The Flesh is strong, and we are weak. Now, make your report in a more fitting manner.'

In a calm, emotionless voice Gentek said, 'The Savages have attacked the main lock. Soon they will gain entrance to the Tower. What must we do?'

In a voice equally calm, Jabel replied, 'You must

fall back gradually. I will have disruptor cannon set up on level twelve. We will trap the Savages there and destroy them.'

13

The Last Battle

Leela and the Doctor reached the corridor outside
the main control room just in time to see Jabel and
Gentek come out and hurry in the other direction.

They pressed against the wall to avoid being seen.
Immediately the lights flickered, and red emergency
lighting came on. The Doctor pulled Leela away.
'You'll have to be quicker than that, you overgrown
adding machine,' he shouted.

The emergency lighting faded and the main lights
came on again.

Deep inside the computer complex, multiple screens
showed images of Leela and the Doctor, and the
Doctor's voice could be heard saying, 'There are probably sensory inputs almost everywhere. He can monitor every tiny change in temperature and pressure,
every vibration ...'

'You did say he was the most powerful computer
ever built.'

'Oh he is, and very charming too, when he wants
to be. Marvellous host. I remember one of his dinner
parties ...'

The pictures on the screens changed as the Doctor and Leela moved away.

In the corridor Leela was saying, 'Doctor, what are we going to do? Xoanon is trying to kill you—and he knows exactly where we are.'

'Ah yes, but we know exactly where he is. Fair dos, Leela, you wouldn't want an unfair advantage, would you?'

'Yes,' said Leela firmly.

The Doctor grinned. 'Somehow I thought you'd say that.' He hurried her into the control room.

On the lower levels, a fierce battle was raging. The Sevateem were through into the main lock by now, and were driving the Tesh back. The Sevateem fought ferociously, using their own primitive weapons, and disruptor guns wrested from the Tesh they killed. Tomas ran to Calib, who was directing operations from a side corridor, Neeva at his side. 'They're retreating, up a kind of steel ladder,' he gasped. 'Going further up into the Tower.'

'Then they're beaten,' said Calib exultantly. 'We shall follow them and destroy them!'

'No, Calib. Something doesn't feel right. It was all too easy.'

Neeva was staring ahead, as if in a trance. 'It is not yet finished,' he whispered.

Calib ignored them both. The success of the attack had convinced him that he was a born general. 'If we let them get away now they'll regroup. We must attack!'

'I tell you it's a trap, Calib!'

'I am the leader—and I say we attack!' Calib turned to the waiting warriors and raised his hand commandingly, 'Forward and destroy the Tesh! Attack!'

Warriors were crowding round now and fierce voices took up the cry. 'Attack! Attack! Attack!' Calib rushed off, at the head of the shouting warriors.

'You fool,' yelled Tomas. 'You'll get us all killed.' But no one listened.

Tomas ran off after the others, and after a moment Neeva followed, his eyes wide and staring. 'It is not finished,' he whispered. He began chanting from the sacred writings. 'And the Tesh stand between the sons of the Tribe of Sevateem and Xoanon ...'

In the main control room, the Doctor opened a panel on the central control console, to reveal a maze of electronic circuitry. He studied it for a moment, then extracted a transparent plastic cube. He held it up to the light, and Leela saw that it was charred and cracked. 'Just as I thought, burnt out,' said the Doctor. He fished through the assortment of electronic spares in his pocket and took out a similar cube and slotted it into place. Immediately there was a hum of power and all the lights and dials and monitor screens in the room lit up. 'That's pretty,' said Leela delightedly. 'What's it all for?'

'These instruments watch and control all parts of

110

the ship, make sure everything's working properly.'

Leela wandered over to a smaller, shielded console in the far corner. 'What does this one control?'

The Doctor glanced briefly at it and said, 'Atomic generators.'

'Why is this red light flashing, Doctor?'

'Leela, I've not time to explain everything now,' said the Doctor impatiently. 'Later on I'll——' he broke off, realising what Leela had said. 'Flashing?' he yelled, and shot across the control room. His hands flickered over the controls on the little sub-console— but the red light went on flashing. 'Xoanon! He's put the atomic generators on overload.'

'What does that mean?'

The Doctor tipped all the electronic spares from his pocket and began assembling them into a complicated structure with the aid of his sonic screwdriver. 'It means I've got about, oh, twenty-four and a half minutes to build a Reverse Memory Transfer Unit and wipe my imprint from Xoanon's brain.'

'And if you can't do it in time?'

'If I can't do it,' said the Doctor grimly, 'the atomic generators will explode, taking us, Xoanon, the ship and about half the planet with them. Effective—but distressingly crude. I'm really rather disappointed in Xoanon.'

Leela stared at him, struggling to take in the meaning of his words. Unless the Doctor succeeded, they were very close to total annihilation.

Under Gentek's command a small group of Tesh were

setting up the disruptor cannons—larger tripod-mounted versions of the hand weapons. 'Check that the sights are correctly aligned,' commanded Gentek. 'There must be no mistake.'

Jabel surveyed the preparations. 'Are the projectors set up so that the Savages will be forced to come this way?'

'Yes, Captain.'

'Excellent. Then all that remains is to project a blank wall in front of the disruptor cannon. When the Savages enter the corridor we'll wipe them out before they know where the beams are coming from ...'

Jabel staggered, putting his hand to his forehead. Something, some other consciousness was invading his mind. He felt a vast, immensely powerful intelligence surging through his brain, taking control ...

Gentek stared at him in concern. 'Is something wrong, Captain?'

'Don't you feel it ... something ... something ...'

Suddenly Gentek too put a hand to his forehead. 'Yes, Captain ... is it ...'

'Communion,' gasped Jabel. 'Communion with Xoanon at last!'

The Doctor had constructed a kind of headset, and was connecting it to a complicated structure of electronic parts. From this central structure ran a long lead with a connecting-socket on the end.

Unable to help, and scarcely daring to speak, Leela looked on worriedly. She saw that the light on the smaller console was flashing more brightly now. It had been joined by others, and by a steadily rising electronic bleep as all over the console dials and gauges moved towards danger-point.

On the doors of the computer complex a face had appeared. It was the Doctor's face twisted and distorted, and it pulsed steadily with an eerie light.

Suddenly Leela touched her hand to her forehead. The Doctor went on with his task, explaining as he worked. 'Nearly done, Leela. It should be possible to re-absorb everything I originally put into the data core. In theory that should leave me unharmed, and Xoanon sane. Unless of course he's too far gone already, or so powerful that he swamps my brain and burns it out ...'

The glowing face on the door began to speak. The words were slurred and guttural at first then the voice became strong and clear. 'Destroy and be free!' It chanted. 'Destroy and be free! Destroy and be free! Destroy and be free!'

Leela took her hand from her head, and her lips began to move. 'Destroy and be free,' she whispered. 'Destroy and be free! Destroy and be free! Destroy and be free!'

Drawing her knife she advanced on the Doctor.

14

Recovery

At the head of their warriors, Calib, Tomas and Neeva advanced cautiously along the corridors of level twelve. They turned a corner and found themselves facing the muzzles of disruptor cannons—cannons with no one behind them.

Tomas held up his hand to check the warriors. 'You see? It's a trap, set by the Tesh.'

'Then where are they?' asked Calib logically. 'They're retreating I tell you. Why else would they abandon the weapons?'

Still worried and suspicious, Tomas shook his head. 'It doesn't make sense ... What's happening?'

'There's only one way to find out,' said Calib. He was about to lead the warriors forward when suddenly he stiffened, putting his hand to his head. His lips began to move. 'Destroy and be free,' he whispered. 'Destroy and be free! Destroy and be free! Destroy and be free!'

Tomas and the other warriors took up the chant. 'Destroy and be free. Destroy and be free. Destroy and be free!' Faces blank, eyes staring, they moved slowly away, zombies controlled by Xoanon's will.

Only Neeva did not move. He stood still, his head on one side, as if he was listening. His face was not blank, it was alive with a kind of mad intelligence. 'I hear you, Xoanon,' whispered Neeva softly. 'I hear you—and I am coming.' He went over to one of the disruptor cannon and lifted the heavy weapon from its stand.

Carrying it with great difficulty he staggered off down the corridor—in the opposite direction to the others ...

The face was bigger now. It glowed more brightly, and the chant was louder. 'Destroy and be free! Destroy and be free! Destroy and be free!'

The Doctor finished his task and looked up—just in time to see Leela's knife thrusting towards his back.

He flung himself to one side and the blade flashed past him, stabbing deep into the console, and cutting across a power cable. There was a shower of sparks and the shock threw Leela across the room. She hit the far wall and slid to the ground. The Doctor took a quick look at her. 'You'll be all right,' he muttered. The bleeps from the atomic generator console were louder now, their note higher and more urgent. The Doctor hurried back to his rigged-up Memory Transfer Unit and put on the head-set. Crossing to the computer terminal that would give him access to the brain of Xoanon. he was about to plug-in the connector when strong hands grabbed his wrists. He was pulled away from the terminal, his arms pinioned behind him. Struggling wildly the Doctor saw that his assailants were a mixture of Sevateem and Tesh. Jabel, Gentek, Calib and Tomas, all mindless servants of Xoanon's will.

The warning bleeps from the generator console rose higher and higher.

The Doctor knew it was no use attempting to talk to his captors.

Instead he called out to the intelligence that controlled them. 'Xoanon, you'll destroy yourself as well as me!'

The huge twisted face glowed brightly and his voice was a demented howl. 'Destroy, free, destroy, free destroy free ...' it gibbered.

Neeva staggered around the corner, struggling under the weight of the disruptor cannon. At the sight of the glowing face, his face lit up with hatred. Swinging up the heavy weapon he screamed, 'Die Xoanon!' —and fired.

For a second nothing happened. Then a beam of power burst from the glowing face. Neeva's body glowed, twisted in mid-air and vanished, utterly consumed by the shattering burst of energy.

At the instant of Neeva's death, Xoanon's control over his servants slackened—just for a second. This second was enough for the Doctor to wrench himself free, and hurl himself at the computer terminal. 'Now, Xoanon!' he shouted exultantly—and seizing the connector, he lunged for the socket.

The great glowing face screamed, 'No! No ... No ...'

Jabel, Calib and the others, under Xoanon's control once more, leaped for the Doctor, but they were too late ...

The Doctor thrust the connector into its socket ... his body arched, and he gave a cry of pain ...

The glowing face on the door screamed too, echoing the Doctor's agony. It shrank to a tiny spot of light and disappeared.

The Doctor fell back unconscious, ripping away the headset in the fall.

Leela moaned and stirred, beginning to come round.

Calib and Tomas, Jabel and Gentek suddenly recovered from their waking trance. Sevateem and Tesh stared at each other in mutual confusion, over the body of the Doctor.

After an age in which he had floated down and down into limitless darkness, the Doctor drifted back to the surface and awoke.

He was lying where he had fallen in the control room, though someone had straightened him out, put a pillow under his head, and covered him with a thin silver foil space blanket.

Leela sat cross-legged on the floor beside him munching cubes of food concentrated from a foil container.

'Hello,' said the Doctor weakly.

'Hullo, I was beginning to think you'd never come round.'

The Doctor struggled to a sitting position, and winced as the movement sent a stab of pain through his head. 'I'm beginning to wish I hadn't.'

'We thought it was probably safer not to move you.'

'How long have I been unconscious?'

'Two days.'

'Two days? Two days? I haven't got time to be lying around here for two days!'

'What happened about Xoanon, Doctor?'

'I explained what I was doing. Weren't you listening?'

'I don't know. I don't remember anything.'

'No, I don't suppose you do,' said the Doctor thoughtfully. 'Well, I removed—I hope I removed—half of Xoanon's dual personality. How is he?'

Leela shrugged. 'Silent. There hasn't been a murmur from him since we found you unconscious. Jabel's people don't dare approach the Sacred Chamber.'

'The what?' said the Doctor sternly.

'That's what they call it.'

'And what do you call it?'

Leela frowned in thought. 'The main computer complex?'

'Better. Go on.'

'I've told them as much as I can but they won't listen to me. Jabel says I'm an ignorant Savage. We have what you might call a guarded truce at the moment.' Leela brought him a beaker of water, and he swallowed thirstily. He gave her back the beaker and started to get to his feet. 'Give me one of those cubes will you?' He took it and started chewing. 'As soon as I get my strength back, we'll go and see Xoanon.'

Leela hesitated. 'Can I ... come inside with you, this time?' Despite the Doctor's influence she found that the thought of seeing Xoanon filled her with a mixture of curiosity and dread.

'Perhaps, Leela, perhaps.' The Doctor reached for another food-cube.

In an amazingly short time the Doctor's extraordinary constitution, together with the effect of the food cubes, restored him to his old self. Still munching the last of the food cubes, he led Leela along the corridor to the computer complex.

Outside the doors a disruptor cannon lay abandoned. The Doctor looked at the weapon, and at the blistering on the doors. 'Maybe that's why Xoanon lost his grip on Tomas and the others. Someone distracted him. I wonder who it was ...'

'They say Neeva went mad. He was threatening to kill Xoanon. And now he's missing. They've searched the ship and he can't be found anywhere.'

'It could have been him ... If he really was mad, it would have made it difficult for Xoanon to control him.' They came up to the doors and the Doctor paused, smiling encouragingly at Leela. 'Perhaps Xoanon himself will tell us.'

He touched the control and the door opened. 'Anybody home?'

There was a moment of silence, then a calm voice

said, 'Ah, Doctor! I have been waiting for you both. Come in please.' The Doctor led the way into the computer complex.

It was a very different place from the one he had seen on his last visit. The central chamber was bathed in a warm clear glow, and all around complex banks of machinery hummed and whirred contentedly.

The Doctor spoke to the empty air. 'How do you feel?'

'I am—whole,' said the voice. As it spoke the lights pulsed gently in time with the words. The Doctor smiled. The voice was one he had never heard before, calm, resonant, mature. Above all, he noted happily, it was not in the least like his own voice. Xoanon's split personality seemed to have been cured.

'And how are you, Doctor?' asked the voice politely.

'Oh, mustn't complain,' said the Doctor hastily. 'I'm fine now, thanks.'

'Good, good,' said Xoanon. 'I'm glad.'

There was a rather embarrassed pause, like one of those moments at parties when no one can think of anything to say.

It was Leela who broke the silence. She had questions to ask Xoanon, and she couldn't hold them back any longer. 'Why did you do it?'

'Could you be more specific?'

'Keep us ignorant and afraid. Make us hate one another.'

Xoanon paused, considering his words, then said sadly, 'I created a world in my own image. I made your people act out my torment. I made my madness your reality.'

'And told yourself you were creating a race of super-humans?' suggested the Doctor.

'That is so. Independence, strength, and courage in the Sevateem. Self-denial, mind-control, telepathy in the Tesh.'

'And hostility and conflict to speed up development,' concluded the Doctor. 'Until you were ready to combine the best qualities of both Tribes.'

Leela thought back over the long struggle for existence that had been the Tribes' fate for her own life and for generations before that. The wars, the hunger, the deaths ... 'That's horrible.'

'Yes, it is,' agreed the Doctor. Gently he raised his voice, addressing Xoanon. 'Isn't it horrible, Xoanon?'

'Yes,' said the voice sadly, 'it was horrible. But now it is over. We are all free, thanks to you, Doctor.'

The Doctor coughed and said modestly, 'Well, it was the least I could do, in the-circumstances. After all, I did start the trouble in the first place.'

'Yours was a mistake anyone could have made.'

'I don't think *anyone* could have made it,' said the Doctor huffily, and Leela laughed.

Xoanon laughed too, and suddenly the Doctor joined in, greatly relieved. Now he knew Xoanon was cured. A sense of humour is the finest proof of sanity.

'Please, sit down,' said Xoanon. Two chairs appeared from nowhere.

Leela jumped back in astonishment, but the Doctor seemed to take Xoanon's powers of teleportation as a matter of course. 'This is nice,' he said cosily, as he settled down.

'Tell me, Doctor,' said Xoanon. 'Where do you think I first started to go wrong?'

After a very long, and to Leela largely incomprehensible conversation with Xoanon, the Doctor finally led the way out of the computer complex and back to the main control room. There they found Jabel, Gentek, Calib and Tomas, who were busily discussing Calib's plan to unite the two tribes.

A furious row was in progress. Jabel's Tesh conditioning was still too powerful for him to show much emotion but he spoke with icily controlled anger. 'The Tesh, my people, would never agree to such a degenerate plan.'

'That plan is necessary, Jabel,' urged Tomas. 'The Tribes must join for mutual survival.'

'I do not agree.'

'We will ask the Doctor's opinion when he returns,' said Tomas.

'Is it wise?' argued Jabel. 'Would Xoanon wish it?'

'An important consideration, Captain,' said Gentek, loyally supporting his leader.

Calib turned away in disgust. 'This discussion is a waste of time.'

Jabel smiled icily at Gentek. 'What can one expect when dealing with Savages?'

Calib glanced at him. 'Watch your tongue, you scrawny mindbender, or I'll break you in two.'

The Doctor cleared his throat loudly and they all turned. 'Ah, gentlemen,' he said cheerfully. 'Democracy in action, I see!'

They all crowded round him. 'What did Xoanon say, Doctor?' asked Tomas eagerly.

'He is anxious to put right the wrong he has done. He has great knowledge and power which he will put at your disposal.'

'Can we trust him?' asked Calib, cynical as ever.

The Doctor held out his hand. In it was a clear plastic box with a red button set in the lid. 'He offers you this, as a sign of good faith. Press this button, and Xoanon's data banks will be erased. He will cease to exist.'

'Another of his promises?'

The Doctor held out the box. 'There's one way to find out.' Calib backed away nervously. The Doctor offered the box around the group. 'Anyone? No? Good! You have to trust someone sometime.' The box vanished from his hand.

Sevateem and Tesh looked uneasily at each other for a moment. Then Gentek said tentatively, 'If the Tribes do merge we must choose a leader ...'

The Doctor began moving towards the door. 'That's not my problem, gentlemen.'

'There's no choice to be made,' shouted Calib. 'I am the leader of the Sevateem and we are the stronger.'

'Perhaps so,' said Jabel coldly. 'But my people of Tesh would never accept the leadership of a mindless Savage.'

Calib's hand went to his knife. 'That is the final insult!'

Hurriedly Leela thrust herself between them. 'I'm a mindless Savage, Jabel, according to you. Yet I have talked with Xoanon.'

Tomas saw a chance of compromise. 'And that makes you the ideal candidate, Leela. You should be our leader.'

'Me?' Leela was astonished. 'But I don't want to be leader. I'm far too unreasonable, aren't I, Doctor?' She turned round. 'Doctor?'

But the Doctor had gone.

15

Departure

The Doctor had just opened the TARDIS door when he heard someone running towards him through the trees. 'Doctor!' called a familiar voice.

The Doctor turned. 'Leela!'

Leela hurried up to the TARDIS, glancing quickly at the open door. 'I thought you might need an escort. The creatures are still out here.'

'You needn't worry about them any more, Leela. The phantoms were merely projections from Xoanon's disturbed subconscious. Now he's himself again, they no longer exist.'

Leela listened. The forest was calm and silent. 'I suppose you're always right about everything?'

'Invariably, invariably,' said the Doctor modestly. 'Well, goodbye, Leela.'

'Doctor—take me with you.'

'Why?'

'Well, you like me, don't you?'

'Yes, I suppose I do like you,' said the Doctor gently. 'I like lots of people, but I don't cart them about the Universe with me. Goodbye, Leela.'

Before he could stop her, Leela darted past him, through the open door and into the TARDIS.

'Come out of there,' shouted the Doctor. 'Out I say!

Come out!' He followed her inside.

Leela blinked a little at the sight of the impossibly large control room, but after her brief acquaintance with the Doctor she was used to miracles.

As the Doctor came through the door in pursuit, Leela ducked round the other side of the central control console. 'Out you come,' said the Doctor sternly. 'And don't *touch* anything.'

Leela saw a large important-looking lever near her hand. She reached out for it ...

'Don't touch that,' yelled the Doctor. 'It'll send us off into the space-time continuum ...'

Leela grabbed the lever and pulled it over hard.

The TARDIS doors closed, the central column began moving up and down ...

... and a wheezing, groaning noise shattered the calm of the forest as the square blue shape of the TARDIS faded away.

The Doctor was off on a new adventure—with a new companion!